'If you wan[t to] around with[...] do with me.[...]

Rhys pulled he[r ...length of] his body, and as her lips parted on a small gasp of shock his mouth captured hers, hot and insistent, his tongue ravaging the sweet moist recesses within a flagrantly sensual exploration.

Surrender won. She was melting helplessly against him. He was arousing her with an expertise against which she could have no defence. She closed her eyes, a soft sigh escaping her lips...a honeyed warmth flowed through her as he caressed her, his touch smooth and firm against her silken skin.

'Please...' Lynne whispered on a ragged sob.

He laughed softly. 'Is that "please stop" or "please go on"?'

'Please...go on,' she begged helplessly.

Susanne McCarthy grew up in South London but she always wanted to live in the country, and shortly after her marriage she moved to Shropshire with her husband. They live in a house on a hill with lots of dogs and cats. She loves to travel—but she loves to come home. As well as her writing, she still enjoys her career as a teacher in adult education, though she only works part-time now.

Recent titles by the same author:

BAD INFLUENCE

HER PERSONAL BODYGUARD

BY
SUSANNE McCARTHY

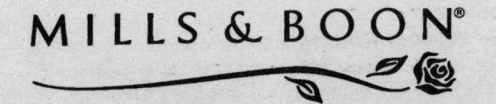

MILLS & BOON®

DID YOU PURCHASE THIS BOOK WITHOUT A COVER?
If you did, you should be aware it is **stolen property** as it was reported *unsold and destroyed* by a retailer. Neither the Author nor the publisher has received any payment for this book.

All the characters in this book have no existence outside the imagination of the author, and have no relation whatsoever to anyone bearing the same name or names. They are not even distantly inspired by any individual known or unknown to the author, and all the incidents are pure invention.

All Rights Reserved including the right of reproduction in whole or in part in any form. This edition is published by arrangement with Harlequin Enterprises II B.V. The text of this publication or any part thereof may not be reproduced or transmitted in any form or by any means, electronic or mechanical, including photocopying, recording, storage in an information retrieval system, or otherwise, without the written permission of the publisher.

This book is sold subject to the condition that it shall not, by way of trade or otherwise, be lent, resold, hired out or otherwise circulated without the prior consent of the publisher in any form of binding or cover other than that in which it is published and without a similar condition including this condition being imposed on the subsequent purchaser.

MILLS & BOON and MILLS & BOON with the Rose Device are registered trademarks of the publisher.

First published in Great Britain 1997
Harlequin Mills & Boon Limited,
Eton House, 18–24 Paradise Road, Richmond, Surrey TW9 1SR

© Susanne McCarthy 1997

ISBN 0 263 80066 0

Set in 10 on 10½ pt Linotron Times
01-9704-63669-D

Typeset in Great Britain by CentraCet, Cambridge
Printed and bound in Great Britain
by Mackays of Chatham PLC, Chatham

CHAPTER ONE

'I AM very sorry, *señora*—there is not anybody at home.'

'But I have an appointment with Señor Santos,' Lynne protested, struggling to keep the edge of impatience out of her voice—the guard on the gate was little more than a boy, and it was hardly his fault if His Excellency the Vice-President Señor José Garcia Santos thought he was so important that he could just forget that he had agreed to this interview, which had been arranged a full ten days ago. 'At five o'clock. My name is Lynne Slater, from the *Daily*—'

'It's all right, Hernando—I'll deal with this.'

Lynne turned, startled, at the sound of a brusque voice close behind her. A pair of grey eyes, hard as steel, were surveying her from a considerable height. At only a little above five feet tall, she was accustomed to having to look up at the world, but this guy was big—six feet and several inches, with an impressive pair of shoulders to match.

'What are you doing here?' he demanded, in a voice that was accustomed to command.

'I'm just. . .' Dammit, why was she letting him intimidate her? She was no cub reporter fresh out of college—this might be her first serious foreign assignment, but she'd had plenty of experience at home of dealing with obstructive boneheads like this. 'Who are you?' she countered, the delicate features that often caused her to be taken for a schoolgirl instead of a woman of twenty-three years set with a grim determination.

Those cold grey eyes flickered with irritation, as if he had better things to do with his time than deal with such a trivial problem. 'Don't get clever, little girl,' he grated, and before she had time to realise what he was going to do he had snatched her tan leather satchel from her shoulder and was searching through it with swift efficiency.

The first thing he found was her tape recorder, and the second was her laminated press pass. 'Lynne Slater,' he read, holding the bag infuriatingly out of her reach as she tried to grab it back. 'That's you?'

'Of course it is.'

He studied the photograph with exaggerated care, as if suspecting a forgery, comparing the image with the reality in front of him. She glared back at him, wishing she had a few more inches to lend her dignity. That cool gaze slid over her in an arrogant appraisal, taking in every detail of the trim figure, from the gleaming crop of blonde hair she had recently had cut elfin-short to the low-heeled sandals on her dainty feet.

'Satisfied?' she queried tartly.

He conceded with a faintly sardonic smile, and glanced again at the press pass. 'I like your hair better long,' he remarked, dropping the pass into the bag and handing it back to her.

Her eyes flashed hot sparks—she might have guessed he would come out with a typically arrogant male comment like that! Long or short hair, it didn't seem to make any difference—men saw a pint-sized blonde and simply refused to take her seriously. But if he thought she could be put off so easily he would very soon find out his mistake, she vowed grimly. She was a professional journalist, and she was here to do a job— and she wasn't going to let some muscle-bound macho throwback stand in her way.

'So—now can I see Señor Santos?' she demanded as coolly as she could manage.

'I'm afraid he isn't here.'

'Will he be gone long?' she persisted, struggling to control her rising temper. 'I could wait.'

'He's out of town.'

'Oh...?' He was lying—she knew it, and he knew that she knew it. 'When did he leave?'

'Yesterday.'

'That's odd,' she responded, arching one finely drawn eyebrow in sardonic question. 'My office spoke to his secretary yesterday afternoon to confirm this appointment, and nothing was said then about him not being here.'

'The secretary made a mistake,' came the blunt response. 'I'm sorry you've had a wasted journey. Good afternoon, Miss Slater.' He turned away from her, indicating to the young guard to open the gate for him.

'Wait! Why did he leave so suddenly?' she pursued, doggedly insistent.

Those cold grey eyes conveyed an unmistakable warning that his sorely tried patience was wearing thin. 'He received an urgent communication—Señor Santos is a very important and busy man.'

The gate had been opened just a few inches, and he stepped through as it was closed swiftly behind him— the young guard was clearly eager to impress. Lynne glared at the man's wide back as he strode briskly up the path, seething with impotent fury. She had met some arrogant types in her time, but he could have won a gold medal!

But, short of storming the gates, there seemed to be little she could do—at least for now. Her hire car was parked a short distance along the pavement, and she went back to it and wrenched the door open with a muttered curse. Damn and blast it! OK, so Paul or David might not have got past that stupid great gorilla either, but at least they wouldn't have had to put up with insulting personal remarks, or that 'little girl' jibe.

She forced herself to draw in a long, deep breath, then breathe out slowly to calm her raging emotions. There had to be a way she could get to see Señor Santos; she had fought too hard for this chance to prove to that bunch of unreconstructed male chauvinists in the newsroom that she was as good as any of them—she wasn't going to give up at the first hurdle.

It had been quite a coup for the paper when Vice-President Santos had agreed to give this interview—there had been rumours of a serious rift with the President, General Elisa. The job should have gone to Paul Coppell, the paper's star reporter, but he was stuck somewhere in Afghanistan with a broken-down Jeep.

Alec had been reluctant to send her—he was of that breed of news editor who was quite happy to let women onto the paper so long as they didn't try to muscle in on any serious male preserve. But with a crucial by-election in Yorkshire, a royal visit to the Far East and a European summit, the resources of the newsroom had been stretched to the limit. Even so, it had only been the risk that any delay might cause Señor Santos to change his mind that had forced Alec's hand.

Bringing her attention firmly back to the job in hand, Lynne took out her tape recorder and dictated a brief outline of what had happened, and then sat back to watch the house. There was no sign of life—the young guard had disappeared into the hut beside the gates. A small frown creased her smooth forehead. What was going on? There had been no indication yesterday that there would be any difficulty about this meeting. And who had that man been at the gate?

From his accent he was definitely English, but his skin had been darkened by the sun and his hair bleached corn-yellow, so he must have been out here quite a while. His clothes—a short-sleeved khaki shirt that had some trouble fitting across those wide shoulders, and camouflage-pattern trousers tucked into a large pair of desert boots—were undoubtedly military in origin, but they bore no insignia of regiment or rank. Some kind of mercenary, perhaps? But whose side was he on? He certainly seemed to think he was the big fish around here, anyway. And that air of cool arrogance was no empty pose—he was not the sort you would care to mess around with.

And, in spite of the derogatory appellation she had bestowed on him, there was something in that weather-hardened face that suggested rather more intelligence than your average bone-headed lump of gristle, she mused. In fact, he was really quite good-looking—if you happened to like that macho type...

But, apart from the obstruction he'd presented, he wasn't her concern, she reminded herself crisply. Where was Señor Santos? He was being hailed as some kind of latter-day Che Guevara, and while she was personally a little sceptical about his new-found moral conscience—he was a politician, after all, and until recently had been apparently quite happy to support the man whom he was now denouncing as a tyrant—his recent pronouncements must certainly have placed him in some danger. Had he been abducted? Or was he still in the house?

A glance at her watch told her that it was after half past five. Soon the swift tropical sunset would bring darkness. She ought to be getting back to the hotel... But not yet. Her heart beating rapidly, she started the car and drove away—as far as the next corner. Then, leaving it in the shadow of a tall casuarina, she crept back towards the house.

An elegant hacienda-style villa, it was built on the hills a little above the hot, crowded streets of the capital—rather a grand residence for someone who wanted to be regarded as a man of the people, Lynne reflected with a touch of cynicism. A high wall, topped with spikes, kept those people out, and she had seen several armed guards prowling the luxuriant gardens when she had peered in through the wrought-iron gates.

There was little point in returning to those gates now—they were locked and guarded, and there was no way of approaching them without being seen. She needed to find another vantage point to be able to look over the wall and catch a glimpse of the house. Glancing warily over her shoulder in case that big gorilla was still on the prowl, she made her way around the block, searching for another gate, an overhanging tree, anything...

There was an empty oil-drum, dumped at the side of the road—it would do. Grunting with the effort, she managed to roll it against the wall, and tip it up. She dirtied her trousers clambering up onto it, but that didn't matter—by standing on tiptoe she could just manage to peer over the wall.

The house was visible through the trees—a long, low white building—but there was no way of reaching it. Doing so would have involved crossing fifty yards of open ground, where a couple of fierce-looking guard-dogs were sniffing around. Disappointed, she was about to drop down again when she spotted a movement at the side of the house—a uniformed chauffeur had come out of a door and was heading towards a side-building that looked like a garage. A moment later she saw a long black limousine appear, and roll slowly round towards the front door.

Of course, he could just be popping out for a packet of cigarettes, she told herself as she skipped down to the ground—but in the official car? Quickly she ran back to her own car and scrambled in, praying that the temperamental engine would start. It was almost dark now; if she was lucky, she wouldn't be spotted—especially if she didn't turn her headlights on.

It was awkward to make a three-point turn in the dark, but she had just managed to get the car facing the right way when the limousine slid majestically past the end of the road, heading away from the town. Leaving as big a gap as she dared, she followed.

There was no moon, just a faint glimmer of starlight to guide her, but fortunately there was little traffic on the road. Ahead she could see the red tail-lights of the limousine, clouded by the dust it was stirring up. They disappeared for a moment as it crossed the brow of the hill, but she soon caught up with it again.

She had no idea where they were going; the landscape was open grassland, bleak and featureless. Blinking her eyes, she struggled to concentrate on her driving—it had been a long flight from London that morning, and the effects of jet lag were making her sleepy. But she had to be careful not to get too close to the limousine—on this empty road there was a danger that they might spot her. She eased her foot off the accelerator, widening the space between them...

A sudden glare of headlights in the rear-view mirror dazzled her. She hadn't noticed another car behind her—it must have been travelling extremely fast. As it pulled out to overtake, she could see that it was a Land Rover, dusty and battered. She slowed to let it pass. If they were in that much of a hurry...

But as it drew level beside her it swung abruptly towards her, forcing her to swerve. With a small gasp of horror she felt the bump as the car left the road, and then she was wrestling with the steering wheel, trying to control a wild skid as the car slewed across the rough grassy scree at the roadside.

It came to rest facing the wrong way, and, wrenching open the door, she scrambled out—even as common sense warned her that it was probably rather stupid to confront her assailant out here on a dark, empty road, miles from civilisation. But the tall figure that climbed out of the Land Rover was unmistakable, even in the dark—and so was the grim expression on his face.

'You!' she spat at him, furious with herself for retreating as he strode towards her. 'What the hell did you think you were doing? You could have killed me!'

He ignored her protest—instead, as she stared at him in surprise, he calmly reached into the car for her handbag and tipped the contents out onto the seat.

'There's nothing in there worth stealing,' she sneered with biting sarcasm. 'You've already searched it.'

'So I'm searching it again,' he retorted obdurately.

He had tossed her tape recorder onto the back seat and was systematically examining the remaining contents—even unzipping her make-up pouch and winding up her new lipstick to its fullest extent, until she was afraid it would break off.

'Careful—it took me ages to find that shade,' she grumbled, deliberately focusing on the trivial in an attempt to disguise the fear that was tying her stomach in knots.

He closed the bag and handed it back to her. 'OK, get in the Land Rover,' he ordered brusquely.

She stood her ground, refusing to be bullied. 'No.'

The shrug of those impressive shoulders indicated total indifference to her defiance. 'Suits me—I'd just as soon leave you here.'

She slanted him a look of surprise—she had been expecting rape and murder at the very least. 'Where are you taking me?' she demanded.

'You'll find out.'

Reluctantly she moved towards the Land Rover. 'This is kidnapping, you know. My paper will make the biggest fuss you've ever heard.'

'Save your breath,' he countered tersely. 'I've done a great deal worse in my time than kidnap some silly little girl who doesn't know when to keep her nose out of places it isn't wanted.'

She would just bet he had. But at least it seemed that he wasn't planning to kill her—if he were, he would have done that right here.

A young man—the one who had been guarding the Vice-President's front gate—had climbed out of the Land Rover and gone over to her car. He started it up, steered it carefully back onto the road and drove off towards the town.

'What about my tape recorder?' she queried, wishing she could make her voice sound cool and confident, as if she were an experienced foreign correspondent to whom things like this were just part of the job.

'You'll get it back. Wait. . .'

She paused as he laid a detaining hand on her arm, glancing up at him in question—and then she drew in a sharp gasp of shock as he turned her so that her back was towards him and with deft efficiency began to pat his hands down over her clothes, from her shoulders to her heels.

For a moment she was too stunned to react, and he calmly turned her around, continuing the search, his hands sliding down over her body with an impersonal expertise that conveyed a total lack of interest in the soft curves beneath his insolent touch. But when he unfastened the top few buttons of her shirt and peered inside—presumably to check that she had nothing concealed in her bra—she was jolted out of her immobility.

She slapped his face so hard that it stung her palm, but he merely returned her a faintly mocking smile, holding the door of the Land Rover open for her. 'Get in.'

She hesitated, but she had little choice but to obey; with her car gone, it would be a very long walk back to town—if he let her go. Quickly buttoning her shirt, she clambered reluctantly into the front passenger seat and fastened her seat belt. There were three more young men in the back, wearing the same kind of military-type uniform as the one who had taken her car, their friendly schoolboy smiles contrasting strikingly with the nasty-looking automatic rifles they were proudly clutching across their laps.

He—she still had no idea what his name was—swung himself behind the wheel, not sparing her another glance as he started up the ignition and drove on down the bumpy road into the empty darkness.

Lynne settled into a bristling silence, staring out through the side window, trying hard to ignore his presence. But he wasn't the sort of man you could ignore—there was an aura of power about him, an uncompromising maleness that she found difficult to handle.

From beneath her lashes she slanted him a covert gaze, studying that strongly defined profile. She couldn't deny that he was attractive—though not as attractive as Paul, of course, with his brooding, Byronic beauty. This was more of a masculine type of handsomeness, hard-boned and rugged—the sort of man that other men would envy and women would want...

Other women, at least—she was spoken for, she reminded herself quickly, twisting the antique garnet ring that Paul had given her for their first Christmas together on the third finger of her left hand. They had been living together for almost two years now—they would be getting married soon... Well, they hadn't actually set the date yet, but it would certainly be some time this year.

They drove for well over an hour, turning off the main road after a while onto an even bumpier one that seemed to lead nowhere. And when at last they came to a halt that seemed to be exactly where they were— nowhere. In the faint glimmer of the moonlight, she could see only rough slopes of sun-baked grassland around them—no sign of life or habitation at all.

The young soldiers had piled out of the back of the Land Rover, and at a word of command from the man-with-no-name they hurried over to something she had taken to be one of the low, scree-covered hills. As she watched in astonishment they began to remove a large camouflage net, to uncover a helicopter.

'What's going on?' she queried, bewildered.

'You wanted to meet Señor Santos,' he responded, a sardonic edge to his voice. 'Well, here he is.'

Another car drew up—not the limousine, but an ancient, battered taxi, one of scores like it on the streets of the city. Three men climbed out of the back— two of them in military uniform, the one in the middle a tall, distinguished-looking man whom she recognised at once from his photographs. Vice-President José Santos. The two soldiers were trying to hustle him along, but he walked with calm dignity towards the helicopter.

The man-with-no-name gestured towards the helicopter in mocking invitation. 'Madam, your flight is now boarding.'

For one crazy moment her mind raced with the possibilities of escape, of telling the world what had happened. But she didn't even know where she was, let alone which was the way back to town. And, though the young soldiers had smiled at her with such innocent friendliness, she had no doubt that they would instantly obey orders to use those deadly-looking weapons they were carrying.

So reluctantly she walked over to the helicopter, and climbed up into the cabin. Señor Santos was already seated, his two-man escort behind him, and to her surprise he welcomed her with a gracious smile.

'Ah, Miss Slater,' he greeted her, his voice calm and polite. 'How delightful to make your acquaintance at last. I do apologise for the unusual circumstances—I'm afraid they are very much beyond my control. Please sit down.'

He gestured to the seat beside him and she sat down, more bemused than ever.

'I regret very much that I was not able to keep our appointment earlier,' he went on, with an urbane charm at startling odds with the desperate circumstances they were in. 'It was at Colonel Carter's insistence... You have met Colonel Carter, I believe?' he added as the man-with-no-name climbed into the cabin, taking the pilot's seat. 'My chief of security. Carter is not his real name, of course, and the "Colonel" is only an honorary rank.'

Sardonic grey eyes met her startled blue ones as he glanced back over his shoulder. 'Fasten your seat belt and put your headphones on,' he instructed her with cool amusement. 'It gets pretty noisy once the rotors start.'

She blinked herself quickly back to action, doing as he'd bidden as he ran quickly through the pre-flight checks and then reached up his hand to switch the engines on. The rotors began to turn, slowly at first, but gathering momentum until with what seemed like an irresistible pull the helicopter lifted to hover just a few feet off the ground, stirring up a cloud of dust from the savannah floor.

Lynne glanced nervously out of the window. She had flown quite often, but only in big jets, never in a tiny helicopter like this. But she wasn't going to let anyone see that she was scared. Surreptitiously she eased her clenched fists, straightening out her fingers and wiping her damp palms on the sides of her trousers.

They rose into the air and banked left, towards a line of hills. Beneath them was only darkness, but she sensed that they were flying low. To escape detection by radar? Clearly Señor Santos wasn't being abducted against his will after all—it seemed that instead he was fleeing the country. A small shimmer of excitement ran through her—this was going to make quite a story!

It wasn't really possible to talk—the headphones didn't deaden all the sound from the engines. She could only try to make herself comfortable and wonder where they were going. At least she had basic emergency supplies in her bag—it was unlikely that she would ever see again the stuff she had left behind at her hotel. Ah, well, there was nothing of any value anyway.

By the time she got home, Paul would be back from Afghanistan. What would he think about her getting this scoop? It would be nice to think he would be proud of her, she mused a little wistfully, but she had an uncomfortable suspicion that he might not be very pleased to find that he had missed out. *He* was used to being the paper's hot-shot foreign correspondent.

Sometimes, even after all this time, she felt as if she was walking on eggshells around him, trying to cope with his changeable moods. One minute he would be the wild romantic, bringing her champagne and whisking her off for a meal at one of their favourite restaurants, the next he was like a sulky little boy.

Especially on the rather delicate subject of setting the date for their wedding.

She did try not to make an issue of it; Paul had been in the middle of a messy divorce when they had first met, and she had accepted, of course, that he needed some space before he would be ready to make such a serious commitment again. But it had been almost two years now—it seemed like a very long time to wait...

In spite of the noise and discomfort in the helicopter's cabin, she was beginning to doze. Yawning, she found her gaze lingering on the man in front of her. Colonel Carter... Who was he really? That look of battle-hardened toughness and easy air of command suggested that he might have been, at least at one time, an army officer, but she doubted that he still was. For one thing, he wore his hair rather longer than any regular army would allow—it curled against his collar like a lion's mane, a slightly darker shade showing through the sun-bleached tips.

A soldier of fortune, then? But what was he doing here in South America, helping a vice-president escape into exile? Such intriguing secrets...

She watched, fascinated, as he eased the controls of the helicopter to take it in a smooth curve around the line of a hill, the hard muscles across his wide back moving smoothly beneath his crisp khaki shirt. She had heard that it took a great deal of skill to fly one of these things, but he seemed to know what he was doing. His hands were strong, but with a light touch on the sensitive controls, almost caressing, coaxing them into obeying his will...

As she slipped slowly into the well of sleep, that thought followed, painting disturbing images in her dreams—images of a hard-muscled male body, a pair of mocking grey eyes...

Lynne had no idea how long she had slept, but she woke with a start as the Colonel's voice came through the headphones. 'We're almost there.'

Was that a glint of mockery in those cool grey eyes as he glanced back at her over his shoulder? But of course he couldn't know what she had been dreaming, she reminded herself quickly, glad of the dimness in the helicopter which hid the hot blush of confusion that had sprung to her cheeks.

She glanced down and saw that they were flying along the line of a river, glistening silver in the moonlight. But which one? Her watch told her that it was almost nine-thirty. Calculating back, that meant they must have been flying for a little over two hours; if she knew their speed she could work out how far they had come, but it must be something around three hundred miles or so—probably the maximum range for a helicopter without refuelling.

A ragged tangle of rainforest ran down close to the riverbanks on each side—there seemed to be nowhere to land. But then suddenly she spotted a small clearing ahead, with a rambling single-storey house built on a low rise of ground—that must be their destination. The helicopter swooped down, and she tensed as the ground rushed up to meet them, but it settled with only the slightest bump and Colonel Carter reached up to cut the engines.

With a sigh of relief she slipped off her headphones and unfastened her seatbelt. Señor Santos had done the same, and now he smiled at her with unruffled serenity, as calm as if the evening's events had been nothing out of the ordinary. 'You will join me for dinner, Miss Slater? Shall we say in half an hour?'

'Thank you.' She shot a swift glance towards his chief of security, but his attention seemed to be fully occupied with the post-flight safety procedures. 'Señor Santos, you agreed to give my paper an interview. Unfortunately the journalist you asked for, Paul Coppell, is unable to make it, but...if you wouldn't mind talking to me instead?'

'But of course,' he agreed graciously. 'Perhaps over dinner, yes? In the meantime, no doubt you will wish to freshen up. Colonel Carter will arrange for you to be given a room.'

Colonel Carter didn't respond, except with a brief flicker of his eyes in her direction. He didn't seem to speak much at all, she reflected acidly. The strong, silent type—no doubt there were plenty of women who fell for that kind of thing, but she wasn't one of them. Besides, she was very happy with what she had—Paul might not quite measure up in the biceps department, but he was sensitive, caring... Qualities which the honorary Colonel would no doubt scorn.

The rotors were still turning slowly as they jumped to the ground, so they had to keep their heads low to run clear. As she straightened Lynne was able to see the house properly for the first time. It was built of wood, with a wide veranda running along the front that had been overrun by a riot of hibiscus, which spilled its fragrance generously onto the warm night air. But there were distinct signs of neglect; in many places the old white paint was peeling away, revealing the bare, weathered wood beneath, and the paved path which led up to the wide front entrance was cracked by weeds.

A small group of soldiers awaited them, wearing the same uniform as the ones who had travelled with them. As Señor Santos came forward the most senior of them rapped a word of command and they all snapped to attention, shouldering their rifles. Señor Santos smiled, greeting them with a few words in Spanish—the pride and pleasure in their response was unmistakable. These were clearly troops who were loyal to him, who had been willing to risk everything to protect him.

'*José! Ah, qué discarso!*' A woman, tall and still beautiful, though no longer young, hurried down the path and into his arms, kissing him on the cheek. 'What a relief! I was so worried—I have been listening to the radio since lunch. Colonel Carter, *le estoy muy agradecido*—I have doubted that even you would be able to bring him safely to me.'

Lynne recognised her as the Vice-President's wife. If the cool demeanour of the man himself had lulled her into the illusion that they had been in no real danger, the relief with which his wife hugged him, and the gratitude with which she thanked Colonel Carter quickly disabused her.

After she had been introduced, and greeted with gracious politeness, she was able to stand back a little and observe the undoubted warmth between Señor Santos and his wife. She had seen many politicians putting on an act of domestic bliss for the benefit of the media, and this was nothing like it. She had already begun to be seduced by his charm herself, she acknowledged wryly—she had better be careful that her article didn't turn out to be an uncritical paean of praise instead of a piece of balanced journalism.

She was able to watch the phoney Colonel, too. He had been greeted almost like one of the family, but it was clear that he regarded himself as being still on duty—there was a quiet watchfulness about him, as if his eyes and ears could penetrate the soft velvet darkness beyond the clearing for any hint of danger. Like a jungle cat, alert to every stirring of the air...

As they walked up the uneven path towards the house, the helicopter took off again, skimming away across the river. Lynne glanced back at it, frowning slightly.

'Don't worry—it'll be back for us tomorrow,' the Colonel assured her, startling her by materialising at her elbow. 'It's just gone to be refuelled. Let me show you to your room.'

'Oh...thank you.' She followed him a little uncertainly into the house. The entrance led into a large but dimly lit hall; here too there were signs of neglect—the upholstery on the two long sofas that faced each other across the middle of the room was faded, the rug between them threadbare, and a large potted palm in one corner was turning brown from lack of water.

He led the way down a gloomy passage, past several

doors, then opened one at the end to show her a small bedroom, clean but rather spartan, with a plain wooden floor and two single beds covered with colourful cotton-weave spreads.

'The bathroom is down the hall,' he told her. 'The third door on the left. Anything you want, just ring for Room Service.'

She chose to ignore the sarcasm of that last remark, simply returning him an icily polite 'Thank you' and closing the door on him.

With a wide yawn she sank down onto the edge of one of the beds; her watch might be telling her that it was barely ten, but her body clock was insisting it was two in the morning. The sleep she had had on the helicopter hadn't exactly been restful, and now she was very tired. But she couldn't fall asleep—dinner would be in half an hour, Señor Santos had said. It would have been nice to change into fresh clothes, but at least she could have a good wash.

The bathroom was as spartan as her bedroom, with an old-fashioned claw-footed bath with big brass taps. But one concession had been made to modern comfort, at least—a shower had been installed over it. She eyed it, tempted... There was no lock on the door, but she would only be a couple of minutes.

Quickly she stripped off her clothes and reached over to turn on the taps. The water gushed out, warm and welcoming, and she stepped beneath it with a sigh of pleasure. It had been quite a day, she mused, letting the warm needles of spray splash down over her body, rinsing away the grit of the savannah from her hair, the weary ache from her bones. At one point she had almost begun to believe it was going to be her last—and though it hadn't turned out like that she doubted that the phoney Colonel Carter would have had many scruples about disposing of her if he had thought it necessary.

An odd little frisson of heat feathered down her spine. She didn't like him—she didn't like his arrogance or his attitude towards her—and yet...she couldn't deny that on a very basic, physical level, he affected her. It was really quite stupid—she had never gone for that muscle-bound, Incredible Hulk type. But there was something in that raw maleness that seemed to arouse an answering core of femininity deep inside her, beyond the reach of reason.

Not that it mattered, she reminded herself crisply. Tonight she would get her interview with Señor Santos, and tomorrow she would be on her way back to London—and Paul. And if she never saw the bogus Colonel again, it would be too soon...

She jerked round sharply as the door opened, gasping in shock and grabbing at the plastic shower curtain to cover herself up. The Colonel himself stood in the doorway, those grey eyes regarding her with lazy mockery. He had a towel in his hand, and his khaki shirt was unbuttoned and hanging open—and suddenly Lynne understood exactly what was meant by the expression to 'go weak at the knees'.

His skin was deeply tanned, liberally scattered with rough, sun-bleached hair across the hard muscles of his chest. Somehow she couldn't seem to breathe as her stunned gaze followed the line of that curling hair as it arrowed down over the ridged plane of his stomach to disappear beneath a thick leather belt. There wasn't an ounce of fat on him—it was all prime beef...

Horrified by her wanton train of thought, she struggled to pull herself together. 'Don't you believe in knocking?' she demanded hotly.

'I'm sorry,' he responded, in the most unapologetic tone she had ever heard, and making no effort to disguise his appreciative survey of what he could see of her body. 'I must have lived too long with only soldiers for company—I'd forgotten the little niceties you have to practise with a woman around.'

She drew in a sharp, angry breath, hugging the flimsy shower curtain closer in a vain attempt to regain a little dignity. 'Pass me the towel,' she demanded, her voice not very steady.

'This one?' He lifted it from the rail, deliberately holding it just a little out of her reach.

'I don't think that's very funny,' she spat at him, sparks of blue fire in her eyes.

'No?' He laughed without humour. 'What if I'm not joking?'

She felt her cheeks go pale. Surely he wouldn't. . .?

His hard mouth curved into a mocking smile. 'All right—there's no need to scream. But if you're going to play in the big boys' league you can think yourself lucky if that's the worst thing that ever happens to you, little girl,' he taunted, tossing her the towel. 'And don't hog the bathroom for too long.'

He went out, closing the door, leaving her shaking, struggling to control her ragged breathing. Damn him—he really was the rudest, most arrogant man she had ever met in her life. But the images his words had conjured would not go away. What if he had carried through his threat, had stepped beneath the shower with her, subduing her struggles with his far superior strength. . .?

Impatiently she shook her head. He had just been trying to frighten her. He really wouldn't have dared. . .Would he. . .?

CHAPTER TWO

THE night was hot and heavy; the ancient fan rotating on the ceiling was doing little to stir the air—Lynne could feel a bead of sweat trickling slowly down between her breasts—and the thick scent of the mosquito coil on the window-sill mingled with the fragrance of hibiscus and jacaranda. Outside the jungle silence was noisy with the chirrup of cicadas and the occasional shriek of a monkey.

In the wood-panelled dining-room, the single glass-shaded globe above the table was reduced to a flickering orange glow as the elderly petrol generator that supplied the electricity spluttered outside. They had finished dinner more than an hour ago, but none of them had moved; Señor Santos was still talking, as Lynne filled page after page of her notebook with her rapid shorthand. There had been almost no need for her to prompt him with questions. He spoke quietly but with deliberation, spelling out a radical programme of reform, every word carrying conviction.

Colonel Carter—she still knew him only as that—was sitting opposite her across the table. He had said little, but she didn't need to look at him to know that he was watching her with those cool grey eyes. It was impossible to guess what he was thinking. Was he remembering their brief encounter in the bathroom? She was finding it difficult to forget—just the thought of it brought a blush of pink to her cheeks.

At last Señor Santos finished speaking, leaning back with a small sigh and briefly closing his eyes. His wife reached for his hand, a small frown of concern creasing her brow. 'You are tired, *querido*?' she asked him softly.

He opened his eyes to smile back at her. 'A little,' he

acknowledged, squeezing her hand with warm affection. He turned to Lynne. 'You have everything you need?'

'Yes...' She closed the pad, stroking her hand thoughtfully over the cover. What was written in there was dynamite—it could bring down a government and send reverberations around the world. 'Thank you.'

'It is I who must thank you,' he insisted, with that smile of gentle serenity which hid an iron determination. 'You can convey my words to where they may count to some effect. We must have the support of the West to end the sale of arms to the present government of my country, who are only using them against our own people.'

She drew in a long, deep breath, all too aware of the responsibility that was now hers—to do him justice in the words she would write. 'I'll try,' she vowed sincerely.

The Colonel made some kind of sound that could have been a snort of scepticism. Señor Santos turned that calm smile to him. 'You have a problem, my friend?' he asked gently.

There was no answering smile. 'It's my job to keep you alive,' he responded grimly. 'I just hope this won't make it any more difficult than it already is.'

Señor Santos nodded his acknowledgement of the younger man's concern. 'That is a risk I must take,' he asserted in the quiet, unwavering voice that underlined his very real courage. 'I owe you my life, and for that I am indeed grateful. But if the price of my life is my silence then my enemies will have achieved their desire without the unpleasant necessity of killing me.'

'They are unlikely to silence you while you're alive,' his wife remarked, with a smile of wry humour that disguised her own quiet courage. 'But *no es asunto de broma*—it is no laughing matter. Now it is getting late, my dear—it is time to bid our guests goodnight.'

He chuckled with laughter, but rose to his feet. 'Indeed. What would I do without you to take care of me?' He turned back to Lynne. 'Goodnight, my dear Miss Slater. It was so very pleasant to make your acquaintance. Goodnight, Colonel Carter—and, once again, thank you for preserving my humble life. I shall endeavour to ensure that it was worth the effort.'

The door closed behind them, and Lynne was left alone with the Colonel. She poured herself another coffee, trying to ignore the unsteady beating of her heart.

'What did you think of him?'

She glanced up, a little surprised that he had spoken—it was the first time he had initiated any kind of conversation since she had met him. 'He's...a remarkable man,' she responded cautiously.

He nodded agreement. 'Very remarkable. He could save his whole country from disaster.'

Slightly encouraged by the opening, she ventured a little gentle probing. 'How long have you known him?' she asked.

'About five years.'

'How did you meet him?'

That hard mouth was a grim line. 'Is this some kind of inquisition?'

'No,' she responded, keeping her voice cool and calm. 'Just background for my story.'

He poured himself another coffee and she waited to see if he would answer her question. The lightbulb above the table flickered—there seemed to be more electricity in the air between them than in the frayed cables tacked to the wooden walls.

At long last he spoke. 'He was Minister of the Interior when I was here with my unit working with the government's drug-enforcement agency. Since then I've been...involved in one or two other things on his behalf.'

'What kind of things?' she asked tensely.

'Pass.'

OK—she knew him well enough by now to recognise that she would be wasting her breath trying to get him to answer any questions he didn't want to. 'You were with the British Army?' she tried instead.

'Yes.'

'Which regiment?'

To her surprise, his eyes slid away from hers, and he seemed to take an inordinate interest in stirring his coffee—though she had noticed he had put no cream or sugar in it. 'You don't need that information,' he responded evasively.

She stared at him, startled. Why should he refuse to answer a simple question like that? Did he have something to hide about his service record? A dishonourable discharge, perhaps? Or had he lied—had he never been in the Army at all? 'Most ex-soldiers are proud of their regiment,' she challenged, a sardonic edge in her voice.

His hard grey eyes regarded her, so cold that she could feel their chill. 'I *am* proud of my regiment,' he asserted quietly. 'Very proud. But they don't need that kind of publicity, and nor do I.'

Of course—she should have guessed! There was only one regiment in the British Army that was as secretive as that—the SAS. They were the élite: the toughest training, the toughest assignments, men who could survive alone in hostile territory for months, if necessary—and kill without compunction. But it was another dead end; she was beginning to think he was the most difficult person she had ever interviewed.

'You've...left the Army now?' she ventured cautiously.

He gave a brief nod of acknowledgement. 'I'm a kind of freelance security consultant. Only instead of guarding banks or shopping malls I guard politicians—or oil wells, or shipments of weapons-grade plutonium.' He smiled suddenly—a smile that hit with the impact of a ballistic missile. 'Anything that looks interesting and pays well.'

It took Lynne several moments to recover from the

effects of that smile. 'You must...get to travel a lot,' she managed at last, her voice a little unsteady.

'Quite a lot.'

'Doesn't your...wife mind you being away so much?' Damn! What crazy impulse had prompted her to ask him a question like that? He'd probably bite her head off...

But he merely shrugged those wide shoulders in a gesture of casual unconcern. 'She knew the situation when we got married.'

So he was married. Well, so what? There was no reason why she should care, she reminded herself sharply. It wasn't as if she wanted to pursue any kind of relationship with him herself—he wasn't her type at all. And besides, she was in love with Paul—she would be getting married herself, just as soon as they could both find a suitable window in their busy schedules. But she couldn't pretend even to herself that her interest was purely professional.

'Do you have any children?'

'No, I don't have any children,' he responded with curt impatience. 'And I'm not going to answer any more of your damned questions.' He rose to his feet. 'It's time to go to bed.'

Her heart kicked sharply against her ribs, and she stared up at him in shock. 'I'm not going to bed with you!' she protested hotly.

He arched a sardonic eyebrow, regarding her with mocking amusement. 'I wasn't suggesting we go together,' he drawled lazily. 'I need a decent night's sleep, and I certainly wouldn't get it with you in my bed.'

She felt her cheeks flame a vivid shade of scarlet. 'That's...just exactly the sort of arrogant remark I would have expected from you,' she threw at him, furious with embarrassment. 'You're not a real officer, and you're *certainly* no gentleman!'

He laughed, those wide shoulders shrugging her attack aside with contemptuous indifference. 'It was you who assumed I wanted to go to bed with you,' he reminded her drily. 'Oh, and by the way,' he added as he strolled from the room, 'if you're planning on taking another shower tonight, you'd better whistle a tune or something. You wouldn't want anyone bursting in on you, would you?'

The clatter of the helicopter overhead woke Lynne sharply from sleep. The pale rays of the early morning sun were filtering in through the broken slats of the window-shutters and for a moment she lay staring at them, fragments of her dreams lingering to confuse her mind. She really was here, in this dilapidated old wooden bungalow somewhere in the forests of South America—that part had been real. The rest...

Shaking her head to dispel the disturbing memories, she skipped out of bed, pausing only to drag on the shirt and trousers she had been wearing yesterday, and padded over to take a look out of the window.

The sight that met her eyes was enough to take her breath away. The house was about fifty yards from the riverbank, surrounded by a fringe of forest—mahogany and cedar, quebracho and Paraná pine. On the far shore the trees made a tangle of dense green, with shreds of morning mist drifting in the hollows as they rose wave upon wave towards a distant grey smudge of mountains—again she wished that her knowledge of geography was up to guessing which mountains they were. The sky was a clear turquoise-blue as the sun climbed lazily above the horizon, not yet hot enough to turn the dewy dampness of the air to steam.

She sighed with pleasure, leaning against the window-frame, breathing in the sights and the sounds and the scents of the rainforest. She hadn't expected when she had flown out from London yesterday that she would have an opportunity like this—but then she hadn't expected any of what had happened.

And least of all had she expected to meet an arrogant swine like the bogus Colonel Carter, she mused wryly.

Oh, she had little doubt that he was good at his job—he would do whatever he had to do, swiftly and ruthlessly—but he was a man who seemed to have little use for women... Except, perhaps, as a sexual convenience when he happened to feel the need, she amended, recalling the predatory way he had looked at her when he had caught her in the shower. She could only feel sorry for his poor wife, waiting meekly at home while he went off adventuring all over the world.

But, though she disliked him intensely, she couldn't deny that strange tug of attraction. It was purely physical, of course, but nevertheless it bothered her slightly—how could it happen, when she was in love with Paul? Perhaps it was just that out here in the wild reaches of the rainforest, so close to the powerful, untamed forces of nature, her rational, sophisticated self had been temporarily usurped by more primitive instincts. Or perhaps it had been the element of excitement and danger in last night's flight that had stirred up those fevered images which had troubled her dreams.

But it didn't matter, she reassured herself crisply. As soon as she got out of here, she would be on her way home. Once she was safely back in England, back to her normal life, she would very quickly forget all about the phoney Colonel...

The sound of the helicopter taking off again cut across her thoughts, and she looked up, startled, to see it swoop over the roof of the house and bank away along the line of the river, the wind from the rotors tossing the tops of the trees like a passing hurricane. With a shout of protest, she darted for the door—that had been Señor Santos she had seen in the passenger seat!

But when she tried to drag the door open, it stuck fast. She rattled it—the wood was old; it could have warped—but realisation was not far behind. It wasn't stuck—it was locked. Fury exploded in a flurry of fists pounding on the unyielding wood. There was only one person who would have done this—Colonel Carter, or whatever his real name was.

Damn him—how dared he lock her in? Her feelings found some relief in a torrent of abuse—working with a bunch of hardbitten male journalists in a busy newsroom, she had picked up a fairly colourful turn of phrase, though this was the first time she had ever felt the need to use it.

The sound of the key turning in the lock silenced her—she had only half expected her tirade to produce any result. The door swung slowly open, and the phoney Colonel himself stood in the doorway, one wide shoulder leaning casually against the frame, a faintly mocking smile curving that hard mouth. 'Where on earth did you learn language like that?' he enquired, sounding more than a little impressed.

'Never mind my language,' she sizzled, wishing with a sudden ferocious aggression that she was big enough to hit him. 'What the hell do you think gives you the right to lock me in?'

For answer, he patted the gun holster he had clipped to his belt. 'This is what gives me the right,' he grated, a sardonic inflection in his voice. 'Do you think this is some kind of Sunday afternoon picnic? We're about a hundred miles from anywhere, and there's no one around but a handful of soldiers who are under my command. So don't make any mistake about it, little girl; around here, at the present moment, my word is law—the *only* law. Do I make myself clear?'

She glared at him in bitter defiance, but even through her anger she was forced to acknowledge that there was absolutely nothing she could do about it—he held all the trump cards. 'Perfectly clear,' she conceded acidly. 'So would you mind telling me what's going on?'

He shrugged those wide shoulders in a gesture of casual unconcern. 'Señor Santos and his wife have just left.'

'So I saw. Why didn't you tell me they were leaving? At least I would have liked the chance to say goodbye.'

'I didn't want you poking that cute little nose in,' he responded, a hint of steel beneath the lazy mockery of his voice. 'The less you know, the better, so far as I'm concerned. He's far from out of danger yet—I don't want you rushing off with the news of his escape until he's safely in the clear.'

Her blue eyes sparked forks of lightning at him. 'You think I'd do anything to put him at risk?'

'I've never known a journalist yet who could resist a scoop,' he countered on a note of dry cynicism. 'That's why I'm keeping you here for a while longer—until there's no chance that you can do any damage.'

'You're *what*?' she demanded explosively. 'You can't keep me prisoner here! That's...kidnapping.'

'So what are you going to do about it?' he enquired with mocking arrogance.

She tilted up her chin, mustering every ounce of dignity she possessed. 'I...I can't do anything,' she acknowledged coolly. 'But my paper will. When they find out I'm missing, they'll raise Cain.'

'You're not missing. Señor Santos's secretary has sent them a fax to tell them you're with him.' He smiled slowly, letting those hard grey eyes slide down over her in an insolent appraisal that set her hackles rising. 'I'm afraid there isn't very much to do,' he taunted softly. 'No newspaper, no television—probably not even a pack of cards. Looks like we'll have to make our own entertainment.'

'*You* can make your own entertainment,' she snapped back at him in cold fury. 'Count me out.' The key was still in the lock and she snatched it swiftly, slamming the door in his face and locking it from her side before he could make any move to stop her. But his only response was a husky laugh.

'What time do you want breakfast?' he enquired.

'I don't want any breakfast,' she retorted to the closed door.

'Suit yourself.' His voice was laced with a maddening

amusement. 'If you change your mind, just come and find the kitchen.'

'Don't hold your breath!'

An enticing aroma of coffee reminded Lynne of how hungry she was. Impatient as a caged tiger, she paced across the room, damning the bogus Colonel Carter with muttered curses, fuelling her anger with a bitter recitation of everything he had done since yesterday afternoon, when he had turned her away from the gates of Señor Santos's villa.

He had won again, she conceded wryly—she would have to give up and seek out the kitchen sooner or later. It would be stupid to starve herself to death. After raking a comb swiftly through her short blonde crop and slicking on a touch of lipgloss, she walked over to the door and turned the key.

The house was eerily silent. The coffee-trail guided her along wood-floored corridors carpeted with threadbare rugs, the walls showing dark patches where paintings and other artefacts must once have hung. Who had lived here? Missionaries? Coffee traders? When had they abandoned the house, leaving it to return to the jungle?

At last she reached the kitchen, and, gritting her teeth to hold onto her anger, she pushed open the door. It was a big room, once probably a hive of activity but now as dusty and neglected as the rest of the house. In the middle of the redundant space was a large scrubbed wooden table that would easily have seated twenty, though now only a couple of broken chairs and a few stools remained.

The Colonel had taken the one good chair, and was tucking into an emperor-sized omelette, light and fluffy and stuffed full of mushrooms. Lynne glanced at it in surprise. 'I thought you said everyone had gone?'

'They have. I cooked this myself. Would you like me to do you one?' The offer could have been taken as perfectly innocent, an olivebranch, but Lynne didn't miss the dark glint of mockery in his eyes.

'No, thank you,' she responded with cool dignity. 'I'm perfectly capable of making my own omelette.'

'Go right ahead,' he invited, waving a hand around the room. 'The eggs are in the fridge.'

'There's a certain logic in that,' she bit out, vinegar on her tongue.

She stalked over to the fridge and took out eggs and milk, and then looked around for a frying pan. A couple of saucepans and an old-fashioned aluminium colander hung from hooks on the wall, but no frying pan. She began to open cupboards, but most of them were empty. Of course, the sensible thing would have been simply to ask the Colonel, but she refused to let herself make that concession—somehow he seemed to have brought out a streak of obstinacy in her that she was sure she had never possessed before she had met him.

He was watching her, that hard mouth curved into a faintly sardonic smile as she worked her way along the row of cupboards, but in vain. There was no sign of a frying pan—but surely he must have used one to make his own omelette? Finally he pointed to a rack above the sink.

'Thank you,' she conceded tersely.

The next problem was lighting the hob. It was run on Calor gas, and it took some fiddling to find the right tap to turn. But at last it was alight, with no assistance from him, and with a smile of grim satisfaction she dropped a knob of butter into the pan to melt and turned her attention to the mushrooms.

Although the room was large, it somehow felt too small for the two of them to be in it. Even when she was trying to ignore him, she was far too aware of him—she could feel him watching her, those grey eyes lingering insolently over her neat *derrière* in the creased cotton trousers. As she sliced fiercely into the mushrooms she was imagining what she would like to do to him...

A spitting from the frying pan warned her that the butter was overheating, and she moved it quickly from the heat while she searched for a bowl to mix the eggs in.

'Cupboard on the left,' he advised blandly.

'Thank you.' She found it, but then cracked the first egg too hard, so that the shell disintegrated and she got goo all over her hand. 'Damn,' she muttered under her breath—she wasn't much of a cook at the best of times, but why did it have to be just when she wanted to appear cool and at ease that she seemed to be all fingers and thumbs? Just let him make one of his sardonic remarks, that was all—just one...

There were no more eggs, so she would just have to make the best of what she had. With a fork she managed to fish most of the pieces of eggshell out of the bowl, and then cracked the other egg more carefully. She stirred in the milk and whipped up the mixture with the fork, then poured it into the pan and added the mushrooms—it was a bit of a soggy mess, but it would be edible.

The Colonel cast an astonished eye over her plate as she brought it to the table. She sat down opposite him, glaring at him, defying him to mock her culinary efforts.

'Er...are you actually going to eat that?' he enquired dubiously.

'Of course,' she responded with dignity. 'What's wrong with it?'

'It looks like it's been hit by a howitzer.'

'I don't usually do much cooking,' she returned with frosty disdain. 'Paul and I usually eat out.'

He slanted her a questioning look. 'Paul? That's your boyfriend?'

'My...fiancé.' The word didn't come smoothly because it wasn't one she usually used—in the rather self-consciously voguish media circles she moved in, it would be thought of as more than a little old-fashioned.

But it gave her an odd sort of satisfaction to be able to use it now.

He arched one eyebrow in patent surprise. 'You're engaged?'

'Yes, I am,' she retorted, indignant. 'What's so strange about that?'

He smiled—a lazy, sardonic smile. 'I had the impression you didn't like men.'

'I like some men,' she countered, letting the hint of disdain in her voice imply that he wasn't included.

Those grey eyes flickered with dark humour. 'So what are your criteria?' he queried provocatively.

She chose to give her answer a measure of consideration he really didn't deserve. 'I like a man who's sensitive, caring—who isn't afraid of showing his feelings. Someone who shares my interests—'

'Like what?'

'Well...the arts, for one thing. The theatre, ballet...'

He made a noise that sounded suspiciously like a snort of disdain. 'This Paul takes you to the ballet?' he protested, his mouth full of omelette.

Lynne returned him a look of withering scorn. 'Yes, he does,' she confirmed with pride.

'He sounds like a schmuck,' he remarked bluntly.

Her eyes flashed with blue fire but she held onto her temper, knowing that he was only trying to needle her. 'You never take your wife to the ballet?' she enquired.

'Not if I can help it.'

'Poor woman,' Lynne remarked with feeling. 'I feel sorry for her—married to a philistine like you.'

'Philistine?' He seemed to be finding the conversation amusing. 'Funny—she used exactly the same word.'

Lynne felt a strange tightening in her chest. For some reason she didn't want to talk about his wife. Not that she cared that he was married, of course—it was just that...somehow it didn't suit her image of him to see him as a married man.

'It seems to me that you're the one who doesn't like women,' she commented with a touch of asperity.

He shrugged those wide shoulders, his eyes smiling mockingly into hers. 'Oh, I like them well enough,' he responded. 'In their place.'

'Oh?' It was almost a struggle to speak. 'And where's that? The kitchen or the bedroom, I suppose?'

He laughed—a low, husky laugh that made her shiver with heat. 'I don't have to bother about the kitchen,' he pointed out, indicating the remains of his omelette with his fork. 'I can cook well enough for myself.'

The tension that had been coiling inside her exploded in a burst of hot fury. 'That's just the kind of crass remark—'

He cut her off abruptly, holding up his hand for silence as the walkie-talkie on the table beside him crackled into life. He picked it up, listening intently for a moment and then returning a message in swift Spanish that Lynne couldn't understand.

'What is it?' she asked, frowning.

'A slight change of plan,' he announced grimly. 'We're clearing out of here—now.'

'Now? But why the sudden panic?' she protested. 'I haven't even finished my breakfast—'

'You're going to have to leave it,' he grated impatiently, grasping her elbow and hauling her to her feet. 'Unless, of course, you want to stand around and argue with a bunch of guerrillas armed to the teeth.'

'But who—?'

'Don't you ever stop asking questions?'

Without ceremony he hustled her out of the kitchen and down the corridor to the front door. A battered Land Rover was waiting at the end of the path, and as he pushed her towards it she heard the distant rattle of gunfire. Abruptly she halted, and though the sound had chilled her heart she shook him off, spinning away to race back up the path towards the house.

'Where the devil are you going?' he demanded, grabbing at her arm again.

'My notebook,' she explained swiftly, evading his grasp. 'I left it in my room.'

'There's no time to go back for that now...'

'I have to get it,' she insisted forcefully. 'It's what I came for—I'm not leaving it.'

'Damn!'

He was hard on her heels as she hurried down the deserted corridors, the thud of their footsteps loud on the darkly gleaming wooden floors. Lynne was already beginning to regret the impulse that had made her come back for the notebook, but its contents were too precious to lose—she had promised Señor Santos that she would do her best to do him justice, and she would never be able to reconstruct his words from memory.

The familiarity of her own room gave it a comfortable air of security, but she was sharply aware that it was an illusion. The sun was higher now, burning the dust in the air. Her notebook was on the bedside table and she snatched it up, tucking it swiftly into her bag. The Colonel had run over to the window, surprisingly light on his feet for such a big man, drawing his gun as he checked around outside.

'I think we'd better leave this way,' he decided. 'It could be too risky to go back now.'

She joined him at the window, peering down. On this side of the building the ground fell away towards the river, and below her was a ten foot drop.

'You...you want me to jump down there?' she protested weakly.

He arched one sardonic eyebrow. 'You'd prefer the alternative?'

'It won't be much help if I break my ankle!'

'You won't break your ankle,' he assured her without sympathy. 'The ground's much too soft. Just keep your feet together, bend from the knees and roll with it as you land.' He smiled suddenly. 'Go on—you can do it.'

'That's easy for you to say,' she muttered mutinously. But it was that or take the chance that whoever had come after them wasn't already at the front of the building. Slanting him a caustic glance, she swung her legs over the window-sill, closed her eyes and jumped.

The ground might have been soft, but the impact as she hit it knocked the breath out of her body. The Colonel landed beside her with a thump, but was instantly on his feet, grabbing her arm and hauling her up, hustling her along in the shadow of the building.

They had almost reached the corner when something whistled past her head—so close that she could feel the pulse of heat—and splintered the old weathered wood a few feet ahead of them. She didn't even have time to scream before she was dragged to the ground and found herself crushed beneath the weight of a hard-muscled male body, staring up into a pair of hot grey eyes.

A sudden jolt of sizzling sexual awareness sliced through her, and for one brief, wild moment she forgot where she was, forgot the bullet that had so nearly taken her head off. She gazed up at him, dazed by the unexpected impact of that raw response, realising with a small shock that he had felt it too. Lying there, sprawled on the damp ground, it was almost as if they were making love...

His face was inches above her own, and she caught her breath at the surge of primitive need inside her, a need that was beyond all sense or reason. His eyes darkened in recognition, and his head bent slowly towards hers as her lips parted softly in anticipation of his kiss...

But then abruptly his expression changed, and he drew back. 'Damn you, can't you ever do as you're told?' he demanded angrily. 'If you hadn't insisted on going back for your damned notebook...!'

'If you hadn't kept me here in the first place...'

Another shot skimmed past, inches above their heads, and Lynne ducked instinctively beneath the protection of his wide shoulder, fear and panic mingling with other emotions that she knew were completely out of place. 'They're *shooting* at us!' she protested. 'They're shooting at *us*!'

'So wave your press card at them,' he retorted, an inflection of sardonic humour in his voice.

She opened her eyes to glare at him, and found that he was actually laughing. He had to be crazy; they were out in the middle of the South American rainforest, miles from anywhere, someone was firing live bullets at them—and he was *enjoying* himself!

'Don't worry,' he assured her with a grin, 'those were just wild shots—they aren't close enough yet.'

'Oh, well, that's a relief,' she spat back. 'Would you mind telling me what the hell we do now?'

'We make for the river.' He eased himself up onto his elbows, peering cautiously towards the place where the gunfire had apparently come from. 'Crawl until you reach that tree with the crooked branch, and then when I say go, run for it. And keep your head down.'

'I was planning to.'

They crept a few yards on their stomachs, and then at the Colonel's prompting nudge Lynne rose to her feet to dart in a crouching run across the rough ground beneath the trees. At every second she expected another hail of bullets, but now she could see the riverbank just ahead—and a small boat, moored at a wooden jetty.

The planks of the jetty were slippery and rotten, and she almost lost her footing as she scrambled onto them, but the Colonel caught her arm and steadied her. They made it to the boat and he pushed her flat onto the deck as he swiftly untied the rope to cast them off, then leapt to the helm. She was terrified the engine wouldn't start, but it fired into life as he pressed the ignition and swung the wheel to take them out into the centre of the current.

With a heartfelt sigh of relief she eased herself up from the deck, peering back over the stern at the receding jetty. A group of soldiers had burst through the trees, their rifles raised to their shoulders, and she ducked again as a volley of shots splashed into the water around them, some of them close enough to bite into the ancient wooden hull.

A sudden grunt snapped her head around. Though they were almost out of range, one bullet had been lucky. As she dived to catch the wheel the Colonel crumpled slowly to the deck, his leg twisting awkwardly beneath him, an ominous scarlet stain spreading across his trousers, mingling with the green and brown blotches of the camouflage pattern.

CHAPTER THREE

FINDING a parking space anywhere near the Fulham Road on a Friday night could be construed as something of a miracle, so, when the Porsche pulled out without signalling, Lynne refrained from giving the driver a rude hand-signal and slipped her beloved little yellow and 'rust' 2CV into the space at the kerb.

It was only the middle of September, but already the summer was gone. It was raining—hard, persistent autumn rain, darkening the grey London pavements. Keeping her head down, she scuttled across the road and along the terrace of neat little Victorian cottages, past the immaculately varnished front doors—each one subtly distinguished from its neighbours, to assert to the world that the proud owner wasn't *just* another wine merchant or gallery-owner or something-in-the-city.

Eight o'clock, Carole had said—she was almost three-quarters of an hour late. Oh, Carole would understand, of course—because even though in the world of glossy magazines, where her elegant older sister worked, deadlines weren't such a frenetic scramble as on a national daily they were still important.

No, it wasn't that which was making her bad-tempered—it was the fact that it had been such a stupid, sleazy story to be chasing in the first place. What had happened to the keen, ambitious young journalist of just a few years ago? The one who had thought she could change the world with a few well-chosen sentences?

The high point of her career had been the interview with Vice-President Santos, just before his successful coup which had toppled the corrupt military dictatorship in his country—she had been nominated for the

Journalist of the Year award for that story. But that was more than a year ago now—since then it seemed to have been all downhill. She was beginning to think she was in the wrong job.

The doorbell buzzed emphatically as she pressed it, and a few seconds later the door was opened by Carole herself. 'Lynne! Heavens, you look like a drowned rat! Don't you have an umbrella?'

'Can't be bothered with one,' Lynne responded, unconcerned, shaking her head to spin the raindrops from her golden-blonde crop. 'Sorry I'm late.' She gave her sister an affectionate hug. 'There's a bit of a flap going on about that Australian actress's libel case—it looks like it's going to be withdrawn.'

Carole sighed, shaking her head, but then melted into a smile. 'I might have known the paper would have to come first! Well, never mind—we've only just sat down. Here, give me your jacket—it's dripping all over my carpet. Come on into the dining-room. You'll know almost everyone here, I think—except...'

It was something in her sister's overly casual tone that gave Lynne the warning. 'Hold on,' she protested, grasping Carole's arm and drawing her back from the dining-room as she was about to push open the door. 'You haven't fixed me up with another of David's dreadful authors again, have you?'

'Of course not... Well...he *is* one of David's authors... Oh, but this one's different,' she insisted pleadingly. 'Just wait till you meet him.'

'I don't want to meet him,' Lynne responded, her blue eyes sparking. 'Carole, you *promised*... Especially after the last one you dished up for me!'

'I know, I know—though, honestly, Peter's a sweetie once you get to know him.'

'He did nothing but drone on and on about writer's block. I nearly stabbed him with the cheese-knife.'

'Well, all right,' Carole conceded wryly. 'But I'm just trying to encourage you a little bit. I do think it's time you got over Paul—it's been more than three months now.'

'I know exactly how long it's been,' Lynne grated. 'And I don't need to get over him, thank you very much—I'm blissfully happy to be rid of him. In fact, being single suits me very well—I have absolutely no desire to find myself in another "relationship".'

Carole smiled with older-sister understanding—though she really didn't understand at all, Lynne reflected with a touch of wry humour. Carole was far too shrewd and sensible to be taken for a ride by a smooth-talking cheat like Paul Coppell—it took a fool like herself to do that.

'Just come and meet him,' Carole pleaded. 'There's no harm in that, is there? Honestly, he's gorgeous—if I didn't have David, I'd snap him up myself.'

'Then why does he need a blind date?' Lynne countered with a touch of asperity.

'Oh, Lynne! It's taken me ages to persuade him to come to dinner. I wanted it to be a surprise—I really thought you'd like to meet him.'

'Why?' Some kind of strange premonition was making the tiny hairs on the back of her neck begin to prickle. 'Who is it?'

She tried to pull her sister back, but Carole had already pushed open the door to the dining-room. 'Here she is, everyone!' she announced with a flourish. 'You know Sebastian and Poppy, don't you? And Julian and Samantha? And *this* is R.J. Hunter.'

Except that was no more his real name than Colonel Carter.

Those hard grey eyes hadn't changed a bit; they regarded her across Carole's exquisitely laid dining-table with exactly the same lazy mockery with which they had regarded her across another dinner table, in a dilapidated bungalow of peeling wood in the heat of a tropical night, fifteen months ago. And the flicker of sardonic recognition in them told her that he, too, remembered.

The last time she had seen him he was being wheeled into an operating theatre in a hospital in San Leopoldo. She had gone off to file her story and to get some sleep—and when she had returned the next morning it had been to discover that he had discharged himself from the hospital and disappeared.

She had wondered, briefly, when Carole had first told her about the mysterious new author David had signed—a former member of the SAS, a soldier of fortune, who always used a pseudonym, who wouldn't agree to be interviewed or photographed... But she had quickly dismissed the notion; she couldn't imagine the man she had known undertaking such a tedious, desk-bound task as writing a book.

She might have expected that he would defy logic, she mused wryly. That first novel—an action thriller with the sharp taste of reality—had been snapped up by Hollywood for some fantastic sum, with an option on the second, which wasn't even written yet. But, damn him, if he'd *had* to become a writer, why had some perverse fate decreed that he should settle on her brother-in-law as his publisher?

Because David was one of the best, of course, but it was just her luck that the first time she met him again it would have to be when her hair was all spiky from the rain and she hadn't had time to do more than throw on the first outfit that came out of her wardrobe! Not that it mattered what she looked like, she reminded herself fiercely—she certainly didn't care what he thought of her.

'Mr...er...Hunter and I have already met,' she managed a little unsteadily.

That hard mouth had curved into a faintly sardonic smile. 'We have indeed,' he acknowledged. 'Good evening, Miss Slater. You'll excuse me for not standing—I have a little...difficulty at present.'

'Oh—you two already know each other?' Carole murmured awkwardly, sensing that her 'surprise' had fallen a little flat. 'How...nice. Lynne, do sit down—

you'll have to hurry to catch us all up; we've almost finished our starter already!'

Reluctantly Lynne took the seat beside him, as Carole was indicating, and struggled to pin some kind of smile in place as she turned to him. 'I didn't know what had happened to you,' she said quietly. 'They told me at the hospital that you had come out of surgery OK, but then you'd discharged yourself against medical advice. I'm glad you were...all right—I mean...'

Her eyes slid involuntarily to the ebony walking stick on the back of his chair; she had endured many pangs of guilt in the past fifteen months, knowing that it was partly her fault that he had been shot—if she hadn't insisted on going back for her notebook... Unfortunately he didn't look like the kind of man who would be very easy to apologise to.

The grim set of his mouth confirmed her assessment. 'It was just a scratch,' he responded in dry tones. 'And a timely reminder never to let a damned journalist get in my way again.'

'I was only trying to do my job!' she protested, stung.

The look he returned her said a few things that would have been very much out of place at Carole's polite dinner party if spoken aloud, and he turned away from her to talk to his other neighbour, who was batting her glitter-tipped eyelashes at him and leaning close so that he could get the full impact of the perfume wafting from her luscious cleavage.

It was as brusque a brush-off as Lynne had ever received, and she felt a faint blush rise to her cheeks and she bent her attention to the dainty parcels of smoked salmon and *crème fraîche* wrapped up with a sprig of chive, over which Carole had expended so much artistic talent. He hadn't changed much since the last time they had met, she mused with a touch of wry humour—he was still the most infuriating, impossible man she had ever met in her life.

Oh, there were a few physical changes—minor ones. From beneath her lashes she studied him with covert curiosity. His hair, no longer bleached by the sun, had darkened to the colour of honey, and he might have lost a little weight—although those shoulders were still impressive beneath the well-cut black dinner jacket he was wearing. But there were faint lines of strain around his eyes, which could have been brought on by the pain of his injuries, and a certain air of weary cynicism, as if he found the niceties of civilian life intolerably tedious.

And he still had that same unnerving effect on her pulse rate. She had told herself frequently over these past fifteen months that it was only the circumstances of their first meeting that had made him seem so...attractive—had they met at a party, or something, she would probably have barely noticed him.

The trouble was that she had let herself dream about him—just a little—believing herself safe from ever meeting him again. And when she had been splitting up with Paul, and her self-esteem had been at its lowest ebb, it had been a kind of escape, a harmless fantasy to imagine herself meeting him again and finding that strange spark of sexual excitement still sizzling...

But fantasies were one thing, real life was another, she reminded herself briskly; quite apart from anything else, there was the small matter of his wife. Fifteen months was more than enough time for things to have changed...maybe even for them to have had a baby... Something discordant jangled inside her, but she didn't care to examine its causes too closely.

She slanted him another thoughtful glance from beneath her lashes. He was taking little part in the conversation around the table; didn't he know that he was supposed to be Carole's star guest? Or was he deliberately playing the strong, silent type, knowing that that would have all the women—and most of the men—vying to engage his attention?

After that earlier rebuff she was a little wary of trying to speak to him again—which was pretty silly, she chided herself impatiently; it was her job to talk to awkward people. 'What made you decide to take up writing?' she ventured with polite interest.

He sent her a cool look from those hard grey eyes. 'I was laid up for a couple of months with my leg in traction, and I didn't have much else to do,' he responded tersely. 'Any more questions?'

She refused to allow herself to be needled; she had interviewed enough reluctant and downright rude subjects to be able to maintain a polite façade. 'Why did you discharge yourself from hospital?' she asked. 'I was expecting you to be in for quite a while.'

'I didn't,' he responded bluntly. 'I had myself moved, and arranged that anyone enquiring for me would be told I'd gone.'

She stared at him in blank surprise. 'Why did you do that?'

'Why do you think?'

Lynne sighed wryly to herself. Maybe she couldn't blame him for being so hostile, she acknowledged fairly; it couldn't have been much fun having his leg almost shattered by a bullet. But it was a little unfair to put all the blame on her; he had kept her against her will at the lodge—if he had let her leave with Señor Santos, she wouldn't even have been there when General Elisa's soldiers had arrived.

'How's your wife?' she persisted, determined not to give up.

'My personal life is none of your business.'

'I'm just trying to be friendly,' she protested, the blunt rebuff stinging through her professional shell.

He laughed in cynical mockery. 'Friendly? You're a journalist, aren't you? You ask questions for a living.'

Lynne felt her hackles start to rise. 'You really don't like journalists, do you?'

Those hard grey eyes returned her a look of icy distaste. 'I value my privacy, Miss Slater,' he stated, his voice very quiet and controlled. 'That's why I've gone to the trouble of concealing my identity by using a pen-name. I should be very grateful if you would respect that.'

'Ah...' So that was what was bugging him—it should have occurred to her that he would assume she was after a bit of celebrity gossip. She shook her head, smiling. 'I'm not planning to do a story on you,' she assured him quickly. 'I don't write that kind of stuff.'

'No?' The arch of his eyebrow conveyed frank scepticism. 'I sincerely hope not. I like David—it would be very aggravating to have to find another publisher, should I find that his wife and sister-in-law had conspired to breach my trust.'

Lynne felt her jaw tighten in anger; he wasn't only accusing her of duplicity, he was accusing Carole as well. 'Your warning is quite unnecessary,' she countered with frosty dignity. 'I wouldn't dream of doing anything so unprofessional.'

'Good.' He turned his attention away from her so pointedly that it was almost embarrassing.

Well, he had certainly made his position clear, Lynne acknowledged with a touch of asperity. Not that she didn't have a certain sympathy; she had always despised the kind of gutter journalists that leapt on their unsuspecting victims like a pack of wolves, transforming them into overnight heroes, hassling their friends and family and generally making their lives hell, only to take equal pleasure in knocking them down as soon as the next cheap sensation came along. But there was no need for him to parade his prejudices at Carole's dinner table!

Fortunately Carole, watchful for any sign of tension between them, intervened swiftly. 'Lynne, come and give me a hand in the kitchen,' she begged.

'Of course,' Lynne responded, her tone pointedly sweet, to emphasise to the man beside her that she was really just an ordinary, warm human being, not some kind of two-headed monster. She rose to her feet, gathering up the plates of those nearest to her and following her sister from the room.

'You really must tell me what you think of this Cumberland sauce,' Carole urged brightly as she bent to load the dirty crockery into the dishwasher. 'It's made with a dash of port—it hasn't even appeared on the cookery pages yet.'

Lynne smiled to herself in secret amusement. Her sister's dinner parties, her clothes, her house—her whole life—seemed to have been clipped from the pages of the glossy magazine of which she was assistant editor. Even her husband looked as if he had stepped straight out of the monthly romantic short story: tall, dark, exceedingly rich and handsome, a successful publisher—and an absolute dear.

It was little wonder that Carole was always trying to matchmake for her friends and acquaintances, Lynne mused drily—she just wanted them all to be as happy as she was. But for some people that just wasn't on the cards.

Oh, she had thought it was for her once; Paul had been everything she had thought she wanted—handsome, intelligent, ambitious... She had met him within a few weeks of coming down to London; he had walked into the newsroom—the paper's star reporter, back from yet another successful foreign assignment—creating a stir of excitement within every female in the room—and he had made a beeline for her.

She had been wary at first—his divorce had still been going through at the time—but he had been difficult to resist, and within a couple of months they'd been living together. It hadn't been quite what she had wanted, but, as he had explained, given his recent history he needed time before he would be ready to make the commitment of marriage again.

And so she had been understanding, and waited...and waited... For almost three years. Three years when she could have been getting on with her life. Three years wasted on that...creep! And then what did he do? No sooner had he got the promotion he had been angling for than he had announced that their relationship was over—a plain hack journalist was no longer good enough for his new image. He was going to marry the glamorous editor of the Sunday supplement!

So it was little wonder that she was off men—with luck, permanently. Especially men like R.J. Hunter—or Colonel Carter—or whatever his damn name was! Oh, she had no doubt that most women would swoon at his feet, wanting nothing more than to let him wipe his thumping great Army boots all over them. But not her. He might not like journalists, but there had been no need for him to behave like such a boor when she had only been trying to be pleasant to him!

Carole was fluttering around the kitchen, whipping up the perfect sauce to accompany the duckling she had cooked. 'How *do* you do that?' Lynne enquired with an envious sigh.

'What, this? Oh, you take the shredded rind of an orange and a lemon—'

'No—how do you get it to come out so smooth? Mine always gloops in the saucepan like a lump of porridge.'

Carole chuckled. 'You never were much of a cook,' she concurred. 'But it isn't difficult, if only you'd take the trouble to learn.'

Lynne shook her head. 'I'm afraid it'd be a waste of time. Though maybe I should start reading your magazine,' she added wryly, slanting an envious eye over her sister's chic jade silk two-piece—the perfect foil for her auburn-rinsed hair. 'I could do with picking up a few new ideas. You always look so smart, and I look like a bag lady!'

'You don't!' Carole protested, genuinely shocked. 'Though I must say,' she added judiciously, 'velvet leggings aren't exactly *in* any more. And if you'd just try something different with your hair, instead of keeping it so short all the time—it's practically a crew-cut!'

Lynne laughed, brushing her hand back through her

blonde crop. 'I like it like this—it's easy to manage. Maybe I'd better just leave the glamour to you, after all.'

'Well, at least you're *starting* to think about the way you look again,' Carole returned sagely. 'That shows you're starting to get over him.'

'It's got nothing to do with Paul!'

'No? Then maybe it's got something to do with Rhys?' Carole suggested, with a hint of smug satisfaction.

'Rhys?' So that was his name. It suited him, Lynne mused tartly. Abrupt, uncompromising—like the man himself.

'You never told me you'd met him before?'

'I didn't know it was the same person,' Lynne responded, carefully indifferent. 'And if you've got any of your matchmaking ideas up your sleeve, you can just forget them. Not only does he dislike journalists in general, and me in particular, but as it happens he's also married—I'm surprised you didn't know that.'

Carole shook her head. 'Oh, no, you don't have to worry about that,' she assured her with a dismissive gesture of one beautifully manicured hand. 'They're getting divorced.'

'Oh. . .?' Why had her heart given such a sharp thud? 'Well, that *definitely* lets me out,' she asserted forcefully. 'I've been down that road once, remember? I've no intention of letting myself in for it again.'

'Ah, we'll see,' her sister responded, maddeningly obdurate. 'At least there's a spark in your eyes again— I haven't seen that since you split with Paul.'

Lynne felt a betraying tinge of pink steal into her cheeks. 'Well, if you want us to get through this evening without an explosion, I suggest you and I should swap seats,' she declared forcefully.

'We can't do that,' Carole protested, shocked. 'Not right in the middle of a dinner party!'

'Watch me!' And, snatching up the bowl of rice, she marched back into the dining-room.

Everyone was far too tactful to comment on the alteration in the seating arrangements. The disadvantage, however, as Lynne quickly found, was that now she was sitting directly across the table from those hard grey eyes—and the glint of cool mockery in them told her that he knew exactly why she had changed places with her sister.

Her new neighbour was Sebastian Spicer, a regular at Carole's dinner parties. A famous theatre critic with a rapier wit, he was accustomed to holding centre stage in any gathering, and Lynne sensed in him a certain irritation that some upstart new author was stealing his thunder.

'So, Mr Hunter,' he remarked in his trademark world-weary drawl, 'how is your latest book progressing?'

There was an infinitesimal pause before the response came in even, measured tones. 'Well enough.'

'What is it about?' Sebastian enquired, his interest deliberately edged with mockery.

'People shooting at each other.'

'How thrilling!' Sebastian seemed quite unaware of the threat of danger in those hard grey eyes. In the polite circles he was accustomed to, no one would have dreamed of silencing his irritating intellectual condescension with a fist, but Lynne wasn't at all sure that the Colonel—she still thought of him as that, in spite of knowing it wasn't a rank to which he was truly entitled—would obey the rules. 'They say people should only write about what they know,' Sebastian wittered on. 'Do you agree?'

'It can be a useful starting point,' Rhys conceded, holding his patience in check with that iron will.

'You really were in the Army, then?' Sebastian queried, arching one elegant eyebrow. 'The SAS?'

'That's right.'

'Oh, my goodness!' breathed Samantha, her eyes sweeping up to his in glowing adulation. 'I've always thought they're such a...*romantic* regiment.'

'It's not very romantic tabbing over the Brecon Beacons in freezing fog with a fully loaded bergen on your back,' he responded drily.

'What rank were you?' Sebastian persisted, his polite façade increasingly brittle—he seemed to see the exchange as some sort of competition between brain and brawn.

That hard mouth quirked into a sardonic smile—he knew exactly what was going on. 'Sergeant.'

'Really?' Sebastian beamed in satisfaction. 'I was quite sure you must have been an officer.'

Rhys shook his head, deceptively genial. 'Not if I wanted to stay in the SAS. Officers are only allowed to serve for three years—plus a second term if they're lucky. Besides, it's no big deal being a Rupert in the Regiment—when you're stuck behind enemy lines with only a nine-milly for company, no one's going to bother saluting you.'

'Well, now, more Cumberland sauce, anyone?' Carole leapt in swiftly to deflect Sebastian before he could make any more sardonic comments. 'Rhys, do have some more—there's absolutely loads of it, and I'd hate to see it go to waste.'

Sebastian, sensing for once that discretion might be the better part of valour, turned to Lynne for conversation. 'So, darling, what have you been up to? Uncovered any nice juicy scandals this week?'

She shrugged her slender shoulders. 'Oh, nothing that's going to shake the world,' she responded with a trace of wry humour.

Sebastian chuckled. 'You know, I detect a very definite down-market trend in that rag of yours lately,' he drawled. 'You want to be careful—you'll be joining the bingo-and-bosoms brigade before you know it.'

'It's happening everywhere,' she responded, feeling a little awkward at being put in the position of defending something she heartily disagreed with. 'It's the pressure of commercialism, I suppose—it brings everything down to the lowest common denominator.'

'And so we must mourn the demise of yet another fine institution,' Sebastian declaimed with theatrical resonance. 'The Great British Press.'

'Oh, I don't think it's quite dead and buried yet,' she argued. She couldn't help glancing briefly across the table at Rhys as she spoke—no doubt these remarks would serve to reinforce his prejudices. Fortunately he seemed to be paying no attention to their conversation; Samantha had finally succeeded in monopolising him, gazing up at him with undisguised adoration—somewhat to the irritation of her husband, who had tried three times without success to catch her eye.

'Lynne's right,' Sebastian's wife put in. 'In spite of television, newspapers still have an important role to play.'

'But do they always print the truth?' someone else argued as the topic was taken up around the table. 'A lot of the time they just seem to make up anything—they have to have a story or the papers won't sell.'

'But they can do good too, sometimes. Like when there's a war—they let us know what's really going on.'

Sebastian waved a hand in airy dismissal. 'Hah! They only tell us what our masters would have us believe—nine times out of ten they get no nearer the front line than the bar of the nearest Holiday Inn. Isn't that so, Lynne?'

'Not always,' she responded, watching Rhys from beneath her lashes. 'Sometimes they do manage to get. . .a little closer than that.'

Suddenly the memory of that brief moment out on that jungle riverbank fifteen months ago seemed more real that the dinner party chat going on around her—so real that she almost expected to hear the crack of rifle-fire. . . Across the table, those grey eyes met hers, and she felt her heartbeat accelerate alarmingly. Was he remembering it too? Or had it been no more than a figment of her imagination that the response had been mutual?

Sebastian had intercepted the brief spark of tension,

and was quick to jump in. 'Ah, yes—we have here an expert from the other side of the fence, do we not?' he remarked. 'Tell us, Sergeant, as a soldier, how do *you* see the role of the journalist in wartime?'

Anyone less thick-skinned would have been aware that the other man had no wish to be drawn into the conversation, but Sebastian's reputation for scintillating wit armoured him against the inhibiting effects of tact. He was gazing at Rhys, bright-eyed, waiting for him to respond.

He took his time, seeming to choose his words carefully. 'If you want my considered opinion,' he responded, his voice quiet but effortlessly dominating the conversation, 'they don't *have* a role—to the soldier on the ground, they're just a damned nuisance.'

Lynne glared back at him with icy indignation. She was acutely aware that everyone had switched their attention back to her, expecting her to defend her profession, but she had to take a sip of her wine to moisten her dry mouth before she could speak. 'Don't you think it's important that...that someone is there to observe, to keep the public informed of what's being done in their name?'

'Ah, yes—the much vaunted "people's right to know"! Always a nice, high-sounding slogan,' he countered on a note of dry contempt. 'Unfortunately, most of the time the papers use it to justify what's really nothing more than cheap sensationalism. The truth is that most people don't care. They sit down to eat their breakfast and read about thousands of people being massacred, then they tut about it for a moment and say something ought to be done, but they've forgotten all about it by the time they've finished their toast.'

That cynical suspicion had crossed Lynne's mind on increasingly frequent occasions recently, but she had no intention of backing down so easily. 'I thought you were fighting to defend freedom and democracy?' she taunted. 'How can you have that if you censor the Press?'

'I'm not talking about censorship,' he ground out, his anger finding a crack in that cool self-control. 'I'm talking about bloody idiotic journalists who have no idea of the dangers, who just cause trouble and get in the way.'

'Particularly *female* journalists, no doubt?' she retaliated, a little surprised to find how much that 'little girl' jibe still rankled, even after all this time.

The hard line of his mouth told her that he had forgotten nothing of their previous encounter. 'That's right,' he grated harshly. 'The men are bad enough, but a woman can be a damned liability to have around.'

'Oh?' With an effort of will she controlled her rising temper, arching one finely drawn eyebrow in delicate enquiry. 'And why is that?'

'Because sometimes they're so damned busy running back to fetch their handbag they don't notice when someone's about to start shooting at them!'

Lynne felt her cheeks flush a heated red. 'I did not go back to fetch my handbag!' she protested, stung to fury. 'I went to get my notebook. And it's that kind of ridiculous, chauvinistic attitude that prevents women from developing their careers. And that doesn't only apply to journalism—it applies to every area of work where women are trying to get involved. They hit a glass ceiling every time, because men are too scared to let them compete on fair terms!'

She became aware of a somewhat bemused silence around the table, and then Sebastian began to applaud. 'Bravo!' he declared. 'An excellent vindication of the rights of women.'

'Coming from someone who can't even match a pair of socks without my help, that's extremely valuable support for the feminist cause,' his wife put in drily, making everyone laugh as the tension dispersed.

Lynne subsided into an uneasy silence, toying with the remains of her dinner. So much for apologising, she reflected wryly—he had managed to goad her into very nearly losing her temper. And so unnecessarily—she could have argued her point much more effectively if she had kept as cool as he had.

Damn him—she should have known she wouldn't get the better of him. He might no longer be in the Army, but he was still the archetypal trained soldier—disciplined, detached, devoid of the weakness of human emotion.

From beneath her lashes she slanted him another meditative glance. What would happen if he ever let go of that iron self-control? It was quite an intriguing thought... And a stupid one, she reminded herself briskly—she had seen far too many sensible women lured by that old myth of still waters running deep only to find that beneath the smooth surface they proved to be disappointingly shallow after all.

CHAPTER FOUR

'WELL, goodnight, darling—and thank you for a simply lovely evening, as usual.' Sebastian laid a dry peck on Carole's cheek and waved a vague hand in farewell as he wafted off into the night, followed by his wife.

'Goodnight...' With a contented sigh, Carole turned from the front door. 'Well, I think that went off quite well, don't you?' she enquired of no one in particular. 'Rhys, can I get you another cup of coffee before you go?'

'No, thank you,' he responded easily. 'But would you mind if I use your telephone to call a cab?'

'Oh, good heavens—you don't need a cab!' Carole protested. 'Lynne can drop you off—can't you, dear? It wouldn't be out of your way,' she added grittily as Lynne's eyes sparked with fury at being so ruthlessly coerced.

A flicker of sardonic humour crossed that hard mouth. 'Well, if you're sure it would be no inconvenience...?'

'Of course not,' Lynne ground out, forced to be polite. 'I'd be delighted.'

'Thank you.' He rose a little awkwardly to his feet, reaching for his cane. 'Well, goodnight, David. I'll be in touch with you about the contracts early next week. Goodnight, Carole.' His smile for his hostess was warm. 'Thank you for a lovely meal.'

'You must come again,' she insisted, putting up her cheek for him to kiss. 'You can't write properly unless you feed your brain, you know.'

He laughed softly, sliding his arm around her waist and giving her a squeeze. 'I could take that as an open invitation,' he teased.

Lynne watched from the doorway, her jaw tense. So

even her happily married sister was susceptible to his charm! Abruptly she turned away, searching through her handbag for her car keys.

It was still raining slightly. 'It isn't far to the car,' she remarked as he joined her on the front step.

'I can manage it,' he returned tersely.

'I meant...because of the rain,' she explained, angry and awkward; she hadn't meant to refer to his bad leg or to sound pitying—he certainly didn't need it. In spite of the fact that he was leaning quite heavily on his stick, he moved with a natural, athletic grace that made it hard to remember that he had been so badly injured.

They reached her car and he cast a slightly sardonic look over it, taking in the rust around the wing, the clutter of junk on the back seat. 'I'm afraid you won't find it particularly comfortable,' she excused it defensively. 'Of course, you can still go back and phone for a taxi, if you'd prefer.'

'Not at all,' he countered, the faintest hint of a smile curving that hard mouth. 'I've travelled in worse forms of transport.'

She unlocked the door for him, watching with instinctive concern as he manoeuvred his stiff leg inside the car. As she hovered on the pavement he glanced up, that familiar glint of cool impatience in his eyes, and pointedly slammed the door. With a wry grimace, she stalked round the car, unlocked her own door and slid in behind the wheel.

'Where to, then?' she asked tautly.

'Piccadilly.'

So much for conversation, she mused with dry humour as she fastened her seat belt and started the ignition, putting the car in gear and turning down towards the Old Brompton Road. For a few moments she tried to maintain a dignified silence, but she never had been much good at that kind of thing—by the time they'd reached the top of the road she was forced to concede.

'Have you seen Señor Santos recently?' she enquired.

'A couple of months ago.'

'How is he?'

'Working too hard.'

'He wrote to me when my piece on him was published, thanking me for doing a good job. I thought that was really nice of him—to take the time.'

'He's lucky he was alive to do it,' he responded grimly.

Lynne nodded. 'If I'd known what was going on. . .'

'What?' He slanted her a sideways glance. 'You wouldn't have been so damned obstinate about getting your interview?' he challenged with undisguised scepticism.

That was what she had been going to say—but when she thought about it she knew it wasn't true. 'No—I'd probably have been even more determined,' she confessed with wry honesty. 'It was much too good a story to miss.'

'Between the pair of you, it's a wonder any of us came out of it alive,' he remarked drily. 'First I had José insisting on meeting up with his wife before he flew on to Washington, then when he found out you'd shown up he insisted I bring you along. If I'd had my way, I'd have left you driving round in circles on the savannah. Or, better yet, dropped you out of the damned helicopter at two hundred feet—though it wouldn't have surprised me if you'd sprouted wings and flown after us.'

She glanced at him, startled by the unexpected flash of humour—to find him smiling back at her. And her heart kicked sharply against her ribs; he had smiled at her like that just once before, and she had never quite been able to forget it. It transformed him from the hardbitten, ruthless soldier of fortune into. . .the man who had featured in far too many of her dreams. . .

'Er. . .?'

'Oh, Lord!' His quiet warning drew her attention to

the traffic lights, which had changed to red; she had to slam on the brakes, jolting the car sharply. His leg knocked against the side of the foot-well and he winced in pain. 'Sorry...'

'It's OK.' He closed his eyes briefly, and when he opened them again his face had relaxed. 'In fact it's a hundred per cent better than it was—they've finally been able to remove the metal pins that were holding the bone together. Now I just have to exercise to build the muscle up, and it'll be as good as new.'

She gave him a swift glance, a little surprised by the revelation after his previous reluctance to talk. 'It...must have been pretty tough—being laid up for so long,' she remarked carefully.

'Not as tough as the alternative. I was lucky they managed to save the leg—at one point they thought I was going to lose it.'

Lynne hesitated. 'Look, I...I know it was crazy of me to insist on going back for my notebook,' she murmured. 'If I hadn't we'd have got away quicker, and...and you wouldn't have got shot.'

'If my men had been a little more on the ball, they'd have spotted the intruders before they got anywhere near us,' he responded drily. 'So I guess we can call it quits.'

A strange kind of forcefield seemed to hover in the air between them—like that night in the bungalow, when they had lingered so late at the dinner table and it had seemed as though they were generating their own electricity. 'Anyway,' she remarked, struggling to lighten the tone, 'if you hadn't been shot you wouldn't have started writing your books, and you'd have missed out on a whole new career.'

He laughed at that. His laugh was as attractive as his smile—low and husky, the sort of laugh you would want to hear again and again... Hey, careful, she warned herself quickly—don't start letting yourself think like that! This was another man in the throes of a divorce, and she did *not* want to get involved.

Not that he had shown much sign of wanting to get involved with her, she reminded herself with a touch of asperity; he didn't even seem to like her very much. OK, there had been the occasional spark—but even that time when she had thought he was going to kiss her he had been very easily able to resist the temptation.

It was fortunate that he couldn't know of the secret role he had played in her dreams for the past fifteen months, she mused, sending him a covert look from beneath her lashes—she would feel a terrible fool if he ever guessed.

He was leaning back in his seat, watching her driving, but after a moment he seemed to accept that the incident at the lights had been an aberration, and began to relax. 'So, I think it's my turn to ask the questions now.' It was a declaration, not a suggestion. 'Tell me about yourself.'

She shrugged her slender shoulders in a dismissive gesture. 'There's not a lot to tell. I grew up in Manchester—my parents are both English teachers.'

'And Carole's your only sister?'

'Yes.'

'Do you get on?'

'Yes, we do,' she asserted, with enough force to let him know she was telling the truth. 'Even though she's nearly ten years older than me, and even though she's always been the glamorous one,' she added, aware that she was gabbling—it made her nervous, having him sitting so close in her tiny car. 'I was always the tomboy. I hated having to wear a dress or a ribbon in my hair— and I *hated* school uniform! I used to take a pair of jeans, rolled up in my school bag, and change into them as soon as I got out of school. It wasn't very easy, though, having parents who were teachers at the same school.'

'I imagine it wouldn't be,' he acknowledged with a touch of dry humour. 'No doubt that's where you developed your ingenuity for finding ways of evading orders.'

She shot him a swift, wary glance from beneath her lashes, that reminder of their previous meeting calling up echoes in her memory, overlaying the hard line of his profile against the lighted shop windows of Knightsbridge with the images of the last time she had ridden beside him in a car, across that dusty savannah plain, fifteen months ago. There was still something grimly uncompromising about the set of that firm, level jaw, the hard glint in his grey eyes. And he still exuded that aura of raw male power that made her mouth feel strangely dry...

What was happening to her? In real life she didn't even go for that macho type, for goodness' sake! And besides, they had absolutely nothing in common. He was a very successful author who had Hollywood moguls eating out of his hand, while she was just a hack reporter who lived in a poky bedsit in the cold end of Deptford.

'Why did you choose to be a journalist?' he asked. 'Following in your sister's footsteps?'

'Oh, no.' She was having to give most of her attention to concentrating on the traffic around Hyde Park Corner as she answered. 'It was what I always wanted to be. I was the editor of the school magazine, and when I left school I managed to get a job on the local paper. I really enjoyed that, but it was a bit limiting, so as soon as I'd finished my training I came down to London—to seek my fortune!'

'So you're a career woman?' he enquired.

She slanted him a sardonic look. 'Why do people always ask that?' she countered. 'No one ever asks a man, Are you a career man? They just take it for granted.'

He laughed with dry humour. 'Point taken,' he conceded. 'So what will you do when you hit that glass ceiling you spoke about?'

'Take a sledgehammer to it!' she vowed with grim

resolution; at least, she would have, once. But lately...she hadn't been so sure. She had been growing more and more disillusioned; sometimes she thought she might even throw the whole thing in, maybe go freelance, or even try writing a book.

But that was pretty much pie in the sky, she reminded herself with a small sigh—she needed to work in order to live. And it was very much the exception for an author to be able to support herself with her writing alone—rarer still to achieve the kind of instant success that Rhys had enjoyed.

Resolutely she brought herself back down to earth. 'OK, this is Piccadilly. Where to now?'

'The Mayfair Intercontinental. Do you know it?'

'From the outside,' she drawled, a note of amused mockery creeping into her voice. 'I couldn't afford to breathe the air in there. Don't you live in a house, like ordinary people?'

'Not very often. My ex-wife has the house as part of the divorce settlement, and I'm in no particular hurry to find another one. And in the meantime, if I'm going to stay in a hotel I might as well be comfortable.'

'Very comfortable,' she accorded drily. 'So the rumours of that Hollywood advance weren't exaggerated, then?'

'That depends on which figure you've read. Some of them have borne about as much resemblance to reality as the story of the tooth fairy. But then you'd know that, wouldn't you?' he added, a sardonic inflection in his voice.

'Are you suggesting that *I* make things up?' she demanded, stung.

'You're a journalist, aren't you? What do they say? Never let the truth stand in the way of a good story? Don't try telling me you're any different from the rest.'

'I wouldn't dream of trying!' she retorted. 'I'd be wasting my breath trying to talk you out of your stupid prejudices.'

'I don't like journalists,' he grated, those grey eyes

as hard as flint. 'So just remember what I said, little girl—I don't want to open the paper in a couple of days and find you've splashed my life story all over it.'

Lynne was almost choking on the heat of her anger. 'You don't listen, do you?' she bit back at him. 'I have no intention of doing a story on you—now or ever.'

'No? So why was Carole so set on having me come to dinner?' His voice was deceptively soft, laced with menace. 'She really put herself out to persuade me. She clearly intended me to meet you.'

Now Lynne could feel a hot blush creeping into her cheeks. Damn Carole and her matchmaking! It was awkward at the best of times, knowing that she was being trotted out for inspection like a stray puppy in need of a home—particularly when the man in question was one she wouldn't touch with a ten-foot pole! But to have to admit to this man, with his hard grey eyes and sardonic smile, that he was supposed to have taken one look at her and instantly decided to relieve her of her single status was going to be extremely uncomfortable.

'She was...trying to pair us off,' she finally admitted.

'Pair us off?' He slanted her a narrow-eyed glance of suspicion.

Lynne nodded. 'I'm afraid she does it all the time. She's on a one-woman crusade to get the whole world happily matched up. It's usually one of David's dreadful authors—there was one who couldn't talk about anything but murder, and the last one was a chap who kept droning on and on about how he was suffering from writer's block!'

His gaze was still sceptical. 'So what happened to your fiancé?'

The colour in her cheeks deepened. 'We... It...it didn't work out,' she stammered awkwardly.

'Ah!'

'What do you mean, "ah"?' she demanded, her eyes flashing sparks.

'He decided he didn't want to get married?'

'We both decided,' she countered defensively—he was the *last* person to whom she would admit the truth. 'We found that the...the demands of our careers created...problems. Besides, marriage is a very outdated institution—two people ought to be able to stay together without being shackled by the inkstains on some meaningless scrap of paper.'

He laughed drily. 'You don't believe in marriage, then?'

'No, I don't!' she asserted, rather too forcefully. 'And even if I did, I'd be perfectly capable of finding a husband for myself, thank you very much.'

'It's your sister you need to convince of that,' he responded on an inflection of sardonic humour. 'She still seems to think you need a little help. How long is it since you and what's-his-name split up?'

'Three months. Not that it's any of your business,' she added, angry with herself for giving away so much more than she had intended to. 'Which turning is it along here?'

'A little further—just before Green Park tube station. You were very quick to delve into my business earlier—you don't like it when the tables are turned, do you?'

'Not when you ask personal questions like that.'

'Why not? It's left here, by the way. Do you have something to hide? Straight on to the end and turn right.'

She followed his directions, distracted by a Rolls-Royce pulling out in front of her in the narrow street, flustered by his probing—was he trained in interrogation techniques? Questioning her like this, when her concentration was elsewhere, was making it almost impossible for her to consider her answers. 'I...of course not,' she protested. 'Just my privacy.'

'Ah—so you do believe in privacy?' His voice was velvet over hard steel. 'Your own, at least.'

'And other people's,' she asserted, trying not to let

him needle her. 'So long as they're not doing anything criminal, or lying to the public.'

He laughed softly, mockingly. 'The guardian of truth, democracy and the people's right to know!' he taunted. 'You look far too young for such a weighty responsibility.'

'I'm almost twenty-five,' she informed him with cool dignity as she pulled the car into the kerb in front of the wide, elegant entrance to the hotel.

'As much as that?' There was a faintly hollow note in his voice, as if he himself were as old as Methuselah—although she was sure he couldn't be much above his middle thirties. Slipping off his seat belt, he leaned across, putting his hand beneath her chin and turning her face towards him, studying it with eyes that seemed to be binding strange spells around her. 'You look about seventeen.'

'I... I... People often say that,' she stammered, suddenly a little breathless. He was so close... There was a subtle, musky scent about him that was doing odd things to her heartbeat. She lowered her lashes in instinctive defensiveness, and found herself gazing instead at his mouth. It really was an intriguing mouth—firm and hard, with a hint of ruthlessness about it. But when he smiled—as he was now—there was unmistakable sensuality...

His thumb brushed lightly over her trembling lips, stirring a strange tingling electricity in them, and as his head bent slowly towards hers she found herself remembering that last time, in the heat of the South American rainforest, with bullets flying all around them. She had thought he was going to kiss her then, but he hadn't...

This time he did—at least, his mouth came down to hers, warm and firm, assured of her acquiescence. And she didn't know what to do. Her instincts told her to reach out and hold him, to let her lips part and invite a deeper exploration, but she was afraid—afraid that that was more than he wanted from her. Afraid that he was kissing her only because she happened to be there, or because she had somehow sent out an unconscious signal that that was what she wanted him to do—not because he felt any strong attraction towards her.

So she sat very still, her eyes closed, all her senses focused on the way his mouth felt on hers, but not allowing herself to respond. The tip of his tongue probed between her lips, sweeping slowly over the sensitive inner membranes, very controlled—it was almost a reconnaissance, as if he was deciding whether or not to go further and explore the soft, moist sweetness within...

But for whatever reason he chose not to, drawing back, that smile now twisted in sardonic humour. 'Goodnight, and thank you for the lift,' he murmured—and then he was climbing out of the car as she stared after him in a kind of daze. He limped up the wide stone steps, still leaning heavily on his cane, exchanging a brief greeting with the black- and green-liveried doorman who was holding open one of the wide glass doors for him.

Lynne drew in a sharp breath, struggling to regain her composure. Damn him—*damn him*! How dared he treat her like that, as if he had been doing her some kind of favour? She didn't even *like* him, let alone want him to kiss her! Did he think, just because Carole had been trying to match her up, that she was lonely and desperate for a man? He wasn't her type, and she was perfectly sure that she wasn't his.

Men! They all thought that they were God's gift to women, that it didn't matter how rude and arrogant and insufferable they were, all they had to do was give you that soulful look and you would melt in their arms like a snowflake in spring. Well, she was through with melting—from now on she was having nothing to do with any of them!

'Men! Sometimes I'd like to line every single one of them up against the wall and shoot them! Oh, I'm so *angry*!'

Carole laughed in uncertain reaction to her sister's ferocious assertion. 'Sit down, and I'll get Lucy to bring us in some coffee,' she urged soothingly, buzzing through on the intercom to her secretary. 'Now, tell me what's wrong.'

Lynne plumped herself down in one of the comfortable chairs in Carole's elegant office looking out over Hanover Square. It was three weeks since that fateful dinner party, and all the trees in the square were dressed up in their autumn colours of russet and gold, but she was in no mood to appreciate the view.

'Paul I'm-the-big-cheese-around-here-and-no-one's-going-to-forget-it Coppell, that's what's wrong,' she announced, sparks of lightning flashing in her eyes. She drew in a long, deep breath, struggling to control the volcanic fury that was raging inside her. 'He fired me.'

'He *what*?' Carole protested, genuinely shocked. 'But...why?'

'Because I won't sell out to the kind of cheap gutter journalism that's all he seems to want these days! The sexual shenanigans of minor TV stars and vicars' wives... That's not why I went into this job! There's a famine in Africa, allegations of corruption in arms deals, a group of victims trying to sue one of the big pharmaceutical companies, but do we report on them? We do not! We trot off to Birmingham to harass some poor broken-hearted woman who's trying to explain to her children why Daddy's not coming home any more, and ask her how she feels about her husband having an affair with some air-brained starlet from some ghastly television soap opera I never even watch!'

Carole blinked at the force of the torrent. 'Well... Yes—I see your point,' she murmured. 'Mind you, I've thought all along it wasn't a very good idea for you to carry on working on the same paper as Paul after you split up. Especially with him now being your boss.'

'Why should I be the one to leave?' Lynne demanded with brittle defiance. 'Anyway, he's been looking for a way to get rid of me ever since he got that promotion—

him and that padded-shouldered bitch he married. Well, they needn't think I'll take it lying down. I shall sue them for unfair dismissal.'

'You've certainly got a good case,' Carole agreed loyally. 'Ah, thank you, Lucy,' she added as her secretary opened the door and brought in a silver tray delicately laid with two china coffee-cups and a jug of cream, and a plate of sinfully tempting brandy-snaps. 'Here, try one of these. They've been experimenting with them down in the research kitchen—tell me what you think.'

Lynne conceded a crooked smile. She had been buoyed up by her anger since her explosion in her ex-fiancé's office earlier in the afternoon, but she was far too realistic not to be aware of the difficulties ahead. 'The trouble is, jobs aren't so easily to be had these days,' she mused wryly. 'And I can't afford to be out of work for too long—I don't have too much in the way of savings.'

'But...what about when you split up with Paul?' Carole protested. 'Surely you must have got a fair share of the flat? You were paying half the bills.'

Lynne shook her head. 'Unfortunately I was stupid enough when I moved in with him not to insist on him putting my name on the deeds. And since we weren't married he was legally entitled to throw me out without a penny—which he did. And I can't afford to sue him.'

'The creep! You're well rid of him.'

'Don't I know it!' Lynne agreed with heartfelt sincerity. 'At least he's made me damned sure I'm never going to let any man make a fool of me like that again.'

'Oh, but they're not all like him,' Carole asserted. 'There are plenty of good ones around.'

'Like your David, you mean? I'm beginning to believe he's a one-off.'

'There are others, if you'd only give them the chance. I thought maybe you and Rhys might have hit it off...'

Lynne shook her head decisively. 'No way! The only way we'd hit it off is on each other's heads! I'm afraid you might as well give up on trying to matchmake for me,' she added, her mouth full of brandy-snap. 'Mmm—these are delicious!'

Getting another job was proving even more difficult than Lynne had anticipated. She must have sent off a couple of dozen letters, but hadn't a got a single interview—most of them hadn't even bothered to acknowledge her enquiry. It seemed that news of her unfair dismissal claim had got around, and no one wanted to risk having anything to do with her. Even people she had thought were her friends seemed suddenly reluctant to take her calls.

Autumn dragged on, cold and wet. She managed to sell a few short articles, but they were barely enough to pay the rent, and her meagre savings were beginning to dwindle alarmingly. She struggled to put a brave face on it over Christmas, which she spent with her parents, but returning to London in the grip of a gloomy winter made her feel ten times worse.

'Well, Happy New Year.' She toasted herself in cheap wine bought from the local supermarket. She cast a jaundiced eye around the dingy little bedsit—something of a come-down from the smart flat she had shared with Paul in the fashionable part of Islington. Last year they had thrown a New Year's Eve party for several dozen friends... Except they hadn't really been friends so much as useful contacts, she acknowledged with wry honesty.

'Bank balance—nil; career prospects—nil; love life...worse than nil!' she enumerated, draining her glass and pouring herself another. 'You, my girl, are going to have to do something drastic!'

Maybe the idea came to her out of the dregs of the wine bottle, but as it sprang fully formed into her mind she almost gasped in shock. Of course—the cottage! Why hadn't she thought of it before? It was perfect! No rent to pay—and she could really make a start on that book she'd been meaning to write for so long...

She and Carole had inherited it five years ago from their grandmother's only brother—a tiny white cottage, with thick granite walls, perched on a cliff overlooking Porthwyk, one of the prettiest little fishing villages on the wild, rocky north coast of Cornwall. There had never been any question of selling it, even though they were only able to get down there on rare occasions. It would probably be pretty bleak at this time of year, but it couldn't be worse than staying here.

Fired with enthusiasm, she went to hunt for some boxes to make a start on packing all her books. She would just take what she could get into the car, and send everything else home to her parents to store—she could ring her mother in the morning and let her know where she was going. David had whisked Carole off for a New Year cruise of the Bahamas, the lucky thing. There was no one else in this big, dirty city who would even notice if she disappeared off the face of the earth.

Lynne sighed with relief as the familiar turning came up ahead of her, the sigh turning into a yawn. It was almost half past ten at night. She had set off at eight o'clock this morning from London, and she should have been at the cottage hours ago, even taking it easy. But the little yellow car had really not been up to the long drive—the primitive electronic ignition had started overheating before she'd got much past Reading, and she'd had to stop every half-hour or so to let it cool down. Nothing had ever seemed more enticing than the thought of a nice hot bath and bed.

But, in spite of her tiredness, she couldn't resist stopping the car for a moment in a lay-by where the coast road bent round before plunging down the steep hill into the village; she loved this view when she came down here in the summer, when the sun was shining on a blue sea and there was no more than a fresh breeze to ruffle her hair.

It was a little different tonight. There was a gale blowing, whipping the angry waves below her into a white frenzy against the razor-sharp rocks and driving the heavy grey clouds swiftly across the dark sky. She shivered, hugging her thick quilted-cotton jacket more closely around her body—not so much from cold as from a feeling of awe at the sheer power of the elemental forces of nature, unleashed and raging.

Yes, she had been right to come down here, she mused, leaning her folded arms against the stone parapet at the cliff edge and gazing out over the stormy sea; somehow this seemed to put it all into perspective—all the stupid, petty conflicts and meaningless anxieties she had left behind. They were all so...insignificant compared with this. She was glad that she was safely on dry land, and not out there somewhere, being tossed around in a boat.

At last, with a sigh, she turned away and climbed back into the car, starting the engine and driving carefully down the steep hill into the village.

Tucked into a sheltered cove, safe from the Atlantic gales raging beyond the headland, the old harbour was quiet at this hour; just a few wooden lobster boats, the last remnants of a once proud fishing fleet, bobbed on their anchors among the luxury cabin-cruisers of the summer crowd. Above it the sturdy little granite-stone cottages crowded tier on tier up the side of the cliff in a jumble of painted window-shutters and grey slate roofs, sliced by the narrow alleyways the locals called 'tags'.

The car's suspension creaked in protest over the uneven cobblestones along the quayside. It was barely eleven o'clock, but there was little sign of life. The cosy white-painted pub on the corner still showed a light at the window, but most of the shops were shuttered— probably for the whole winter, she reflected wryly; many of those picturesque stone cottage were second homes now, beyond the pockets of local young people, who'd had to move away to find work. She had often thought it was a shame—though not without a twinge of guilt, knowing how much she enjoyed being able to come down here herself whenever she liked.

The narrow streets twisting up from the harbour had not been designed for cars, and she had to drop into second gear, the little two-stroke engine labouring doggedly up the steep slope. Turning left past the lifeboat station, she noticed a couple of cars parked outside; a light still glowed in the window there too. So some poor souls were in trouble out there in that filthy weather, she reflected with a shudder—she could only hope they got back safely.

The cottage stood alone—the last one before the end of the village. It was reached by a flight of rough stone steps cut down the face of the cliff itself—only the grey slate roof was visible from the road. With a sigh of relief she pulled the car over onto a patch of gravel beside the top of the steps and clambered stiffly out.

Maybe she'd give the bath a miss for tonight—all she felt like doing was falling straight into bed. But first she was going to have to unload all her stuff from the car, and take it indoors; common sense told her that down here it would probably be perfectly safe to leave it until morning, but years of living in London had ingrained habits of security in her that had become almost instinctive.

She had been expecting that the cottage would be ice-cold, so it came as a welcome surprise to find that it was warm. She smiled in wry self-mockery—Mum must have rung the local woman who kept an eye on the place for them, and arranged for her to come up and light the Aga, guessing that she would forget to call herself.

Mrs Penrose had obviously dusted round as well— the cosy little sitting-room was spotless. The cottage was a pleasant jumble of rooms opening out of each other, on several different levels. When they had first inherited the place from their great uncle Sholto it had been stuffed with furniture, but they had got rid of most of it, keeping only the best pieces.

A wooden staircase rose to the upper floor, where there were two bedrooms; the third they had made into a bathroom—Uncle Sholto had used a tub in front of the fire even when he was in his late eighties, but they had felt the need of a little more comfort.

At the side was a small terraced garden, from where you could look down on the whole village nestling around its pretty harbour, with the wood-clad hills rising steeply above it—a picture of timeless character and charm. In the summer, the garden was a riot of wind-sown flowers, but at this season there were only a couple of empty terracotta pots, looking a little sad.

But it wasn't the weather to linger there tonight—and besides, she was tired to the point of exhaustion. Surrendering to a wide yawn she turned reluctantly from the view, and dragged herself back up the steps to fetch the rest of her stuff from the car.

She had noticed a computer on the table in one of the smaller rooms; so Carole—or more likely David—had broken their joint resolution never to bring work down here, she reflected with a fond smile. That was handy—her laptop was useful, but it would be easier to use the bigger model if she was going to be working for long stretches.

By the time she had unloaded everything and taken some of it upstairs, she was almost asleep on her feet—it was all she could do to make herself a mug of cocoa to take up to bed. Mrs Penrose had made up the wrong bed, but she was too grateful that she didn't have to do it herself to quibble over that—she could sleep in Carole's room tonight. The tiny bathroom had been tidied too, the towels folded neatly on the rail and the shaving things David had left behind lined up on the shelf with a military precision that made her smile.

She couldn't be bothered to find a nightdress—she couldn't even remember which bag she'd packed them in. Yawning, she slid between the sheets in just her knickers; almost midnight, the little clock on the bedside table told her. Well, she didn't have to be up early tomorrow—or the next day, or the next... But she was going to have to be disciplined if she was going to get this book written, she reminded herself firmly; she had enough savings to last for about six months, if she was careful, but she couldn't afford to let herself get lazy.

Finishing her cocoa, she tucked herself down beneath the quilt and closed her eyes. But just as she was sinking thankfully into the deep, dark well of sleep something began to nag at the fringes of her consciousness. There was something wrong—something in the cottage. Something seemingly inconsequential, but significant. What was it?

Impatiently she punched the pillow into a more comfortable shape and snuggled down, curling up her knees. If she couldn't remember it, it really couldn't be that important. She'd investigate tomorrow...

It was that dream again—she had dreamed it many times over the past eighteen months, but tonight it was somehow even more vivid than usual. She was trying to run, fleeing some kind of unknown danger, but her legs felt heavy, numb. And then she was falling, over and over down a long slope, to land in a tangle of arms and legs, staring up into a pair of hot grey eyes...

She moaned softly, turning over in bed and hugging the pillow, but she didn't wake. His strong arms were around her as he kissed her, caressed her, and she was responding helplessly, the sensually evocative male scent of him fuelling the aching hunger that was gnawing at her body...

The sound of the front door slamming loudly brought her abruptly awake, disorientated. Before she had time to remember where she was, the sound of thundering footsteps on the stairs made her jerk up in alarm, and the next instant the bedroom door was thrown open and the light turned on—and she found herself staring into those same hot, dangerous eyes she had just left behind in her dreams. Except that they were flaming now with anger, not desire.

'Out!' he ordered without preamble. 'Get out of that bed, and out of this cottage—now!'

CHAPTER FIVE

LYNNE stared in bewilderment as dreams and reality, past and present swirled together in a confusing vortex of images. Was she in her uncle's cottage in Cornwall, or on some lonely riverbank in South America with a phoney colonel? 'What. . .? But. . .' Suddenly she realised that the quilt had fallen away, and she snatched it up to cover her naked breasts. 'How dare you?' she protested, blushing furiously. 'Go away—get out of my bedroom.'

'This is *my* bedroom—though I'm sure I don't need to tell you that. And I don't want you in it. I don't know what you think you're up to—'

'What *I'm* up to? I'm not up to anything—I was fast asleep. It's. . .two o'clock in the morning.'

'I'm perfectly well aware of what time it is,' he grated impatiently. 'And I want to go to bed.'

'You can't!' she protested, slithering back in alarm and clutching the quilt to her throat.

Rhys laughed without humour. 'I seem to remember we had a similar conversation once before. I'm sorry to disappoint you once again, but I have no designs on your honour—at this moment I'm afraid I have neither the energy nor the inclination. Now, you have exactly two minutes to get dressed and get out of here.'

'No way!' she retorted with heated indignation. 'You're not the law around here now, you know. I don't have to jump up and salute you.'

He let that mocking gaze drift down to where her hand was clutching at the quilt. 'Now that could be an interesting idea,' he conceded lazily. 'Another time, maybe.' He picked up the clothes she had left in an untidy heap on the chair and tossed them onto the bed. 'Your two minutes have started.'

Lynne grabbed at her sweater, dragging it on over her head, and leapt out of bed in time to see him pick up the bags she had left in her own bedroom and start down the stairs.

'Hey—what do you think you're doing?' she protested, livid with rage. She grabbed at the strap of her big nylon sports-bag, full of clothes, which he had slung over his shoulder. 'Leave my things alone. How dare you?'

'Look,' he growled, those hard grey eyes glinting with menace, 'I came down here for some peace and quiet—the last thing I want is some damned journalist crashing in on me after some kind of stupid story. Least of all you!'

'That again! I told you before, I've no intention of doing a story on you.'

'No? Then why *are* you here?' he enquired with frank scepticism.

'I. . .' She felt a hot blush rise to her cheeks; she didn't want to tell him that she was trying to write a book—as a very successful published author, he would no doubt treat the idea with scorn. 'I'm here to. . .work,' she finished lamely.

'Well, you can find yourself somewhere else to do it,' he warned. 'Your two minutes is up.'

He tugged the bag out of her grasp, but she snatched at it again—and found herself falling as she missed her footing on the stairs. His reaction was instantaneous—dropping the bags to catch her in his strong arms—but he was already off balance, and her impetus was enough to topple him over and send them both tumbling down the rest of the stairs.

For a long moment Lynne lay shocked and winded, enjoying the unexpected pleasure of being wrapped up in his arms; it was just like that day, so long ago now, when he had saved her from the sniper's bullet. . . But as reality reasserted itself she scrambled quickly to her feet.

'I'm sorry—are you all right?'

'Of course I'm all right,' he responded impatiently, levering himself up from the floor. But as he put his foot down he winced in sudden pain, reaching for the newel post at the bottom of the stairs for support.

'Oh, Lord—your bad leg!' Lynne gasped anxiously. 'You haven't broken it again, have you?'

'No, I have not,' he grated through clenched teeth. 'It's the other one.'

'Should I...ring for an ambulance?'

He shook his head, glowering at her fiercely. 'I told you, it isn't broken. I've just twisted my knee.'

'But even so... Shouldn't you see a doctor?' she persisted, acknowledging with a small stab of guilt that—again—it was partly her fault that he had suffered an injury. 'I could drive you to the hospital...'

'I'm not letting you drive my car—on your form to date you'd probably have us straight over a cliff!'

'As it happens, I'm a very good driver,' she retorted, stung. 'Not that I'd want to drive *your* car, anyway.' It was probably a huge great Mercedes or BMW or something. 'My car's outside.'

'That old boneshaker?'

'Well, all right, don't go to hospital, then,' she returned, knowing she sounded petulant. 'It's your leg.'

He drew in a long, deep breath, evidently struggling to bring his anger under control. 'All right,' he conceded tautly. 'We'll go in your car. Thank you.'

'Where's your walking stick?' she asked, glancing around for it.

'I don't use it any more—I haven't needed it for months,' he responded tautly. 'Though, if I'd known you were going to show up again, I'd have kept it!'

'Well, you had no right to try to throw me out like that,' she asserted, refusing to accept all the blame. 'This is my cottage—at least, half of it is.'

He glanced down at her, frowning. 'I thought it belonged to Carole and David?'

She shook her head. 'No—Carole and me. It was left to us by our great-uncle Sholto. And Carole didn't tell me you were here,' she added grimly. She could guess why not—Carole had known she wouldn't like it. And Carole wouldn't have been expecting her to come down here at this time of year, so in normal circumstances she would never have been found out.

Those hard grey eyes regarded her with a sardonic glint. 'And you're telling me that when you arrived and found the place occupied you just calmly took off all your clothes and got into bed?'

'I didn't realise it *was* occupied,' she argued, her cheeks faintly pink. 'I thought it was Mrs Penrose who'd lit the Aga, and there was nothing lying about to show that anyone had been living here—no coffee-cups or newspapers or anything...'

'I prefer to tidy up after myself—unlike you,' he responded drily, his gaze passing over the jacket she had discarded on the sofa, the shoes she had left on the floor. 'But you must have gone into the bathroom?'

'Yes, but...I thought that was David's stuff.' She frowned, searching for the thought that had been trying to impinge on her consciousness as she'd been falling asleep. 'The refrigerator! I just assumed that Mrs Penrose had stocked it up. But, of course, she'd have left a *full* bottle of milk...!'

'Quite.'

'I was tired,' she protested. 'It just didn't register. Besides, it was a very selfish thing to do—trying to turf me out in the middle of the night. Where was I supposed to go?'

He conceded something that could have been a smile. 'All right—I apologise. I wasn't in the best of moods. We've had a very rough night because of some stupid idiots who thought it would be fun to go sea-fishing in this weather and then wanted to put their damned boat above their own lives and ours when it was obvious it was going onto the rocks.'

She stared at him in blank astonishment. 'You mean you were out on the *lifeboat*?'

He nodded, that same stone-wall expression on his

face that had warned her before not to ask questions he wasn't going to answer. 'OK, let's get going. Are you sure you're OK to drive all that way?'

'I'm not tired now,' she assured him—and it was true. The events of the last fifteen minutes had generated enough adrenaline to chase her tiredness away. It was an effect she had often noticed when she was after a good story—she could keep going for days on the minimum of sleep as long as the excitement lasted. After that, of course, she would flake out until she had caught up on what she had missed.

'Perhaps you'd better put some more clothes on first,' he remarked drily, letting his eyes slide down over her slim legs beneath the long, loose sweater. 'If you walk into the hospital like that, they might start wondering how I came to fall down the stairs.'

'Oh...' She glanced down at herself, the colour flaming into her cheeks again—the sweater was only just long enough to be decent. 'Yes, of course, I...won't be a minute.'

She flew up the stairs, her heart pattering rather too fast. Which was stupid, she chided herself fiercely—'I have neither the energy nor the inclination'. You couldn't get much clearer than that!

And that was exactly the way she wanted it. Colonel Carter—or whatever his name was—might be safe enough in her dreams, but in real life he could be disconcertingly difficult to handle.

In spite of her confident assertion that she wasn't tired, Lynne could have done without the long drive down dark, narrow country roads that twisted and plunged like a big dipper. Her passenger didn't say a word, but she could guess that he wasn't finding it a particularly comfortable ride.

They were just a few miles short of their destination when the engine began to miss.

'What's up with it now?' he enquired, in the tone of

one whose patience had long since passed its outer limits.

'The ignition's overheating. We just have to stop for a while until it cools down.' She managed to coax it along to the next lay-by. 'I'm sorry.'

He leaned back, closing his eyes wearily. She slanted him a sidelong glance, able to study him for the first time since they had met again. Apart from the evident strain around his mouth, he looked a great deal better than he had at Carole's dinner party—almost as fit as that day, now nearly eighteen months ago, when she had confronted him at the gates of Vice-President Santos's palatial villa.

He still wore his hair rather longer than most regiments of the British Army would tolerate, and it curled around his ears and over his collar. His jaw was beginning to show a dark hint of stubble too, where he hadn't shaved since yesterday morning—a harshly masculine contrast to the soft silkiness of his lashes as they lay against his cheeks.

Suddenly she felt an aching urge to reach out and touch him. All this time she had been weaving that secret dream around him and now he was here beside her, solidly in the flesh... But if the man she had created in her dreams had burst into her bedroom to find her lying naked in bed he certainly wouldn't have reacted the way *he* had, she reminded herself with a touch of wry humour. What a pity that reality had had to intrude; she would have much preferred to be left with her romantic fantasies—foolish as they might have been.

She cast him another wry glance. It was so difficult to know how to start a conversation with him—most of the usual kind of questions she might have asked, which anyone else would have taken as simple, friendly interest, he was likely to regard as evidence that she was probing for information.

'Have you been to Cornwall before?' That seemed about as neutral as she could get.

'A few times, when I was a kid,' he responded, yawning. 'I had a friend at school whose family had a house down here, and they'd often invite me to stay for the holidays.'

'You...didn't spend the holidays with your own family?' she ventured cautiously.

'The Brigadier was often stationed abroad. From when I was eight, I stayed at school in England.'

'The Brigadier?' she queried, startled into forgetting her intention to avoid personal questions.

A narrowed slit of metallic glitter showed as he opened his eyes. 'My father. Retired now, of course.'

'Oh...' She lapsed into silence for a moment, a little shocked by the bleak image of his childhood that had been conjured up. 'Your father was in the Army too, then?'

'My father, my grandfather, my great-grandfather... As far back as you care to go.' He laughed with a touch of dry humour. 'Unfortunately I didn't quite follow the family tradition in the way that was expected of me. I should have applied for a commission in the family regiment—instead I chose the SAS.'

'What did...your father think of that?' she enquired, watching him carefully for those now-familiar warning signs. But a hint of a smile hovered at the corners of that hard mouth.

'He damned near went ballistic,' he chuckled reminiscently. 'Fortunately my brother Simon obliged in my place—he's a major already, and looking set to outrank my father before he's finished.'

It sounded like a case of 'like father, like son', Lynne mused wryly—apparently the old man expected unquestioning compliance with his orders too. 'You just have the one brother?' she asked.

'One brother, one sister—married to a Lieutenant-Colonel.'

'And your mother...?'

'She died when I was ten.' That sardonic gaze turned towards her. 'Shouldn't you be taking notes?'

She shook her head quickly. 'I'm sorry—I. . .I didn't mean to pry.' She hadn't expected that he would reveal so much of himself. 'It's just. . . Well, you're not exactly the world's greatest conversationalist, you know.'

He looked genuinely surprised at that. 'Aren't I?'

'No, you're not.' She slanted him a tentative smile. 'Getting blood from a stone would probably be a good deal easier.'

'I'm sorry.' Something that looked almost like genuine amusement glinted in those cool grey eyes. 'I hadn't realised I was as bad as that.'

Lynne felt her heart suddenly begin to beat faster; it was still there, that spark. . . 'It's probably habit,' she murmured, her voice not quite steady. 'First being in the Army, and now writing.'

'I don't write all the time. I spent six months on the first book, and then took a six-month contract assessing security on oil installations in Kazakhstan.'

'You must have had some wonderful company there!'

'A tobacco-chewing Georgian who thought Stalin was badly misunderstood,' he acknowledged on an inflection of sardonic humour.

Her blue eyes danced merrily. 'And now you've chosen to tuck yourself away in Cornwall in the middle of winter!'

'So have you.' The suspicion was back in his voice. 'It's a bit of a strange time to take a holiday, don't you think?'

'It. . .isn't exactly a holiday. I. . .needed to get out of my place in London—I. . .I couldn't afford the rent. As a matter of fact I'm. . .out of work,' she finally admitted, flickering a wry glance across at him.

One level eyebrow lifted in quizzical enquiry. 'You resigned?'

'I was fired.'

'Oh?'

'I didn't agree with the editorial policy,' she explained with all the dignity she could muster.

He laughed in lazy mockery. 'Don't tell me—it was an affront to your journalistic integrity?'

'Yes, it was, as a matter of fact,' she retorted, her anger sparking. 'But there's no point arguing with you—you've made up your mind that all journalists are tarred with the same brush, and I don't suppose anyone's *ever* made you admit that you were wrong about anything.'

'Oh, it's happened now and then,' he conceded, smiling enigmatically at her.

Suddenly it felt rather too hot in the car, and, leaning forward, she tried the ignition; it complained a little, but started—at least there wasn't far to go now.

'Ah, good—it's decided to co-operate,' the Colonel remarked in saccharine tones. 'We might get there and back before lunchtime after all.'

She returned him a look of icy disdain. 'There's no need to make sarcastic remarks about it,' she returned loftily. 'At least it's got more character than all those modern things—the only way you can tell most of them apart is by the badge.'

It was fortunate that Lynne had anticipated a long wait at the hospital—she wasn't proved wrong. First there was the wait for the doctor to come, and then an even longer wait for them to take a couple of X-rays. Now they were back in the casualty department again, waiting for the doctor to come back and tell Rhys what the damage was.

Rhys Gillam-Fox... She had finally found out his real name—she had heard him give it to the nurse when they had arrived. Which meant that his father was Brigadier Gillam-Fox—scourge of modern architects and planners. Quite a background! No wonder he had flipped out when his son had joined up as an enlisted soldier!

She could almost envy him now—at least he was able to lie down, even if it was only on a hospital trolley. The hard plastic chair she had to sit on wasn't very comfortable at all, but she was able to lean against the wall, and in the warm atmosphere of the casualty department it was difficult to stop her heavy eyelids drifting down...

An unpleasant mish-mash of images was spinning through her mind—dreams made up of echoing fragments of the noises around her jumbled with distorted memories of the day. There was an uncomfortable sense of guilt as she tried to make amends to Rhys for some unremembered but serious wrong—but everything she did just seemed to make things worse. The last image was of that confrontation on the stairs, and she woke with a start as she felt herself falling.

From the trolley opposite, a pair of cool grey eyes regarded her with mocking humour. 'Thanks for the company,' Rhys remarked. 'You've been snoring for the past half-hour.'

'I don't snore!' she protested hotly, embarrassed at the thought that she had probably been sitting there with her mouth lolling stupidly open, the way people did when they slept sitting up.

'You do. Well, it's more of a kind of snuffle, really—like a little dormouse all curled up in the corner. What were you dreaming about?'

'Nothing!' she responded, a little too quickly—the last thing she wanted was for him to guess that she had been dreaming about him.

Fortunately at that moment the doctor returned. 'Well, the good news is, you don't seem to have done yourself any serious harm,' he announced breezily. 'No bones broken, at least. The bad news is that you could have damaged the cartilage. I'm going to try splinting it to stop it twisting, and you'll have to keep your weight off it for a while—with a bit of luck, that should do the trick. But I'm afraid you'll be off the boat crew for a while.'

Rhys nodded, the grim set of his mouth the only sign of the frustration he must be feeling. 'I'll give Curran a ring in the morning—well, in a couple of hours,' he amended wryly, glancing at his watch. 'We didn't stand down till half-one, so any shout today'll go down to Padstow.'

'OK. I'll have the technician come and fix you up with a plastic splint—it only fixes with Velcro, so you can take it off when you have a bath. Do you want anything for the pain?'

He shook his head. 'No thanks, it's OK. I've lived with worse.'

The doctor smiled grimly—he had seen the scars that testified to many past injuries. 'I dare say you have. But a body can take only so much bashing about, you know. Maybe it's time you started taking better care of yourself.'

Those hard grey eyes glinted with sardonic amusement as he slanted a glance at Lynne. 'I thought I had,' he remarked. 'But trouble has a habit of showing up when you least expect it.'

Lynne returned him only a frosty glare—she wasn't going to rise to that one. The doctor hurried away to deal with another patient, and a few moments later the technician arrived to fit the splint, chatting away with a cheerfulness that made Lynne's head ache.

'There we go—nice and tight,' he announced, hauling on the last strap. 'I'll leave you to get dressed—your wife can give you a hand, eh?'

Lynne sat up sharply at that. 'I'm not—'

'I'm sure she will,' Rhys cut across her smoothly, his smile laced with sharp mockery. He swung his bare legs over the side of the trolley, balancing on the metal hand-crutch he had been given, and picked up his jeans. 'Won't you—darling?'

'I'm not his wife,' she insisted on informing the bemused technician, snatching the jeans grudgingly and shaking them out with a snap. 'Come on, then—put them on.'

She had to bend down to his feet to help him, while he put his hand on her shoulder to steady himself. He's enjoying this, she reflected bitterly, a little too conscious of the hard muscle in his legs, the rough smattering of male hair over his weathered skin. The scars from that old bullet wound, and the operations that had followed, were still visible, though well-healed now, but it wasn't those which drew her eye—it was the well-cut dark blue silk boxer shorts, close-fitting around his lean hips, sparking her too-vivid imagination and making her mouth go dry...

Stop it, she warned herself sharply; he was far too perceptive not to notice her reaction. And, in spite of his apparent dislike of her, she had no doubt that—like most men—he would be ready enough to accept the opportunity for a little casual diversion if it appeared to be on offer.

And she was all too afraid that she might be vulnerable; it was a long time since a man had held her, kissed her, made love to her...too long. But providing that sort of entertainment for the phoney Colonel Carter was not the way to mend the damage Paul's betrayal had wrought—afterwards it would just hurt even more.

A sudden sting of tears pricked the back of her eyes, and she struggled to blink them back—the last thing she wanted to do right now was let him see her crying.

With a casual movement that made her swallow hard, Rhys zipped up his jeans. 'Right then—let's go home... Hey, what's the matter?' he queried, with a sudden soft concern that almost tipped her right over the edge.

'Nothing.' She sniffed and ran the back of her hand briskly across her eyes. 'I'm just tired, that's all. It took me the best part of fifteen hours to drive down here yesterday, and I'd only had a couple of hours' sleep when you burst in on me.'

He laughed in gentle mockery, stroking back a wayward curl of gleaming blonde hair that tended to fall across her forehead. 'Poor Lynne. All right, we'll take a taxi home—you can come back for your car tomorrow. Frankly, I'd prefer to do that anyway—I could do with a bit more room to stretch my leg out.'

He meant he could do with a rather more comfortable ride, she surmised swiftly, but she wasn't going to argue with him—she could think of nothing she would rather do than sit back and let someone else drive them home. 'OK,' she agreed, nodding. 'I'd better just go and make sure I've locked the car up properly if I'm going to leave it in the car park.'

He laughed aloud at that. 'You don't seriously think anyone's going to steal that rust-bucket, do you?'

'It isn't a rust-bucket,' she retorted, automatically springing to the defence of her beloved little car. 'It's only got a few spots here and there. And you never know what some people might steal.'

Lynne awoke at around noon to find the winter sun filtering through the pretty yellow curtains of her bedroom. She slipped out of bed and padded over to the window, letting go her breath in a long, deep sigh of satisfaction as she gazed out at the view.

The sky was a pale winter blue, and the touch of sunshine brought to life the pastel colours of the cottages, jumbled all over each other up the steep, tree-clad slopes. Down in the harbour the bright paintwork of the boats was reflected in shimmering patterns on the sparkling water, while beyond the shelter of the cove the ocean was a tranquil grey-green, mockingly innocent, as if incapable of unleashing the kind of savage display she had witnessed last night.

And Rhys—the Colonel, as she still tended to think of him—had been out in that, she recalled with a shudder. Small wonder that he had been on such a short fuse when he had got home and found her in his bed. Perhaps, under the circumstances, his reaction had been forgivable after all.

But whether or not she would ever forgive Carole for letting him stay here without telling her, she wasn't so sure! A wave of heat shimmered through her as she remembered that moment when he had woken her so abruptly from her sleep. It was strange that she should have been dreaming about him—and yet...maybe not so strange. He had been sleeping in that bed, and the musky scent of his skin must have been lingering on the sheets, invading her unconscious senses—making the dream even more vivid than usual.

And then there had been that ride home in the taxi early this morning. She was sure that when she had dozed off to sleep she had been leaning against the window on her side of the back seat—but when they had drawn up outside the house and he had gently woken her she had found that she had somehow slid across, and was leaning against him, nestled into the curve of his arm.

Refusing to let herself dwell on that memory, she unzipped her bag, and sorted herself out some clothes for the day, and then padded through to the bathroom. It was very much a case of 'His 'n' Hers' in here now, she reflected with a smile of wry amusement. On the left-hand side of the bathroom shelf his razor, shaving brush and shaving foam were lined up in rank formation with a can of male deodorant and a nearly new toothbrush. The toothpaste was neatly squeezed from the bottom of the tube, and the top was firmly screwed onto the bottle of plain and sensible shampoo.

The right-hand side, by contrast, was unmistakably hers: a jumble of bottles and jars, representing a decidedly haphazard approach to skin-care. Her toothbrush was looking a little frayed, and her toothpaste bulged in all the wrong places. Hastily she tried to effect some improvement, wiping the jars over with her flannel and setting them straight on the shelf, hiding the one with the chipped top behind the others, but it really didn't help a great deal.

Pulling a face at her reflection in the mirror, she shrugged her slim shoulders. She was simply not by nature a tidy person—life always seemed too short. No doubt that would be yet another bone of contention with the phoney Colonel, she mused, wryly surveying the intimidating neatness of his side of the shelf. Well, dammit, it was her house—she was entitled to be as untidy as she wanted to be!

But though her thoughts were defiant, the blue eyes that gazed back at her from the mirror held an oddly wistful look. It was difficult to imagine the sort of woman that he would be attracted to having a bathroom like this, she mused wryly; hers would be neat and feminine, all delicate creams in dainty pots—and with one of those glass bowls filled to the brim with cotton-wool puffs. And not a speck of dust in sight.

That was the kind of picture she had painted of his ex-wife—a sweet, fragrant creature, doe-eyed and gentle. What had gone wrong between them? Had he found it too constricting, to settle down to the dull domesticity of marriage after living a more or less bachelor existence in the Army and then as a soldier-of-fortune wherever he could sell his services?

But she didn't particularly want to think about his ex-wife at the moment—breakfast was more to the point. With that worthy intention in mind, she marched across to the other bedroom and tapped breezily on the door. 'Good morning—or rather good afternoon,' she said to announce herself. 'What do you want for breakfast?'

He grunted awake, instantly alert—a soldier's training, she reminded herself as she stepped back in momentary alarm, wondering if he was going to leap out of bed and attack her. But it wasn't only that which made her heart pound so hard—it was seeing him lying there, where she had lain the night before, his dark blond hair rumpled and his wide, muscular chest bare.

'I...er...can do you scrambled egg,' she offered, struggling to tear her gaze from the crisp, curling male hair scattered across that exposed breadth of weather-hardened skin, which trailed down in a thin line to his navel and beyond... Oh, Lord—wasn't he wearing *anything*?

'Thank you.' He grinned wickedly, running his hand across his chest—knowing exactly what she was thinking. And then he sat up, casually flicking back the quilt—and he was still wearing those dark blue silk boxer shorts. She breathed out in an unconscious sigh of relief, giving far too much away. He lifted one dark eyebrow in lazy mockery. 'Military training,' he explained. 'When you're in action, you never know when you may have to get out of bed in a hurry—and a man's pretty vulnerable in the nude.'

'I...suppose so,' she agreed, her mouth dry. Just at the moment, he wasn't the one who was vulnerable. 'I'll...go and sort this breakfast out, then.'

She escaped quickly, hurrying downstairs to the kitchen where she could have a few moments to recover her equilibrium, safe from the disturbing sight of him—even if she wasn't safe from her own overheated imagination.

Firmly controlling the wayward track of her thoughts, she opened the fridge and took out a box of eggs and a bottle of milk, then found a saucepan in the cupboard. Once she had whipped up the mix for the scrambled eggs and set it over a low light, she got out some bread and popped it under the grill for toast. She was just filling the kettle when there came a loud roar from the bathroom.

In a panic, she darted up the stairs two at a time—to find Rhys standing in the doorway, her toothpaste in his hand. 'Did you *have* to decorate the sink with this?' he demanded. 'It has a top—a very clever little gadget—designed to keep the paste *inside* the tube, instead of dripping all over the porcelain.'

She let go of her breath in an angry snort. 'Is *that* all?' she retorted crossly. 'I thought you'd fallen over or something.' She snatched the tube from him, flipped the top back down, and stepped past him into the bathroom to wipe up the tiny white blob of paste with her flannel. 'There!' she grated through clenched teeth. 'Does that pass muster—*sir*? Or would you like me to scrub the floor with my toothbrush while I'm at it?'

'It looks as if you already have.... What's burning?'

'Oh, my Lord—the toast!'

She raced back down the stairs to see a thin wisp of smoke coming out from under the grill. Snatching up a dishcloth, she dragged out the rack, to find two squares of blackened charcoal. 'Oh, damn and blast it!' she muttered furiously under her breath, knocking them to the floor with her finger. Quickly she reached for another two slices, and pushed the grill-rack back into place while she turned her attention to the scrambled egg.

She must have put too much milk in it or something; even to her own eyes it looked disgusting—pale and watery. She found a slotted spoon in the drawer and did her best to drain off the whey, but when it was sitting on the plates, atop the toast which she had finally managed to cook properly, even she had to admit that it was not going to win her a cordon bleu award.

'Well, it's his own stupid fault—making all that fuss over absolutely nothing,' she asserted fiercely. 'Just let him say one word, that's all—just one!'

She was carrying the plates over to the table when he came down the stairs, a little awkwardly as he favoured his injured leg. He was wearing the jeans he had worn yesterday and a dark blue lumberjack-style shirt, his hair slightly damp at the ends from his shower—and looking so casually, compellingly male that it almost took her breath away.

Hey, be careful, she warned herself quickly. Don't start getting to like this—seeing his things in the bathroom, cooking for him and looking after him. She would have to let him stay for a day or two—she could hardly kick him out when it was at least partly her fault that he was injured again, and not able to walk. But after that she would have to insist that he found somewhere else to stay.

And besides, she never had been the domesticated type. That had always been Carole's territory. Lynne was the tough cookie, the hard-nosed reporter who always put the job first. Except she didn't have a job any more—or a man to put it before. Just a handful of stupid dreams that could get her into serious trouble if she didn't get a grip on herself.

She slammed the plates down on the table, her eyes sparking a defiant challenge. He read the warning, contenting himself with a wry glance at the contents of his plate and a polite, 'Thank you.'

'I'm...afraid it's not all that good,' she confessed with masterly understatement. 'I'm not much of a hand at cooking—I leave that kind of thing to Carole.'

'I see.' His face was devoid of all expression—except for a tiny twitch at the corner of his mouth which might have been suppressed mirth. 'Well, thank you for making the...effort.'

'You don't have to eat it if you don't want to,' she said grudgingly. 'I could do you something else.'

'No—thank you. This will be fine. Though I think tomorrow I might, perhaps, stick to cornflakes.'

'Right.' Finally she had to laugh herself. 'I'm sorry—I made a total mess of it.'

'I interrupted your concentration, yelling about the mess in the bathroom,' he acknowledged. 'After all, it *is* your cottage.'

'Yes, but... Well, I really ought to try to keep things a bit tidier,' she admitted. 'Carole's always telling me off for the same sort of thing.'

'Perhaps we could agree a truce?' he suggested, a wry inflection in his voice. 'After all, we're both adults. I need a place to stay for a while, and this cottage suits me very well. We don't need to get in each other's way. If it's a question of paying rent...'

'Oh, no, that's not a problem,' she responded quickly. 'It's just...I mean... All right, I'll...think about it.' Dammit, what was she saying? She ought to be insisting that he leave at once—well, as soon as his knee was better, at least. But somehow, when he was around, she couldn't seem to focus her mind properly.

'Good.' His grey eyes were smiling at her across the

table. 'So, if you'll try to remember to put the top back on your toothpaste, I'll try not to yell at you when you forget.'

She returned the smile a little uncertainly; she wasn't too sure about this pleasant mood—it felt a good deal safer when he was angry with her. 'All right—I'll try,' she agreed. 'I can't make any promises, mind—I'm always full of good intentions where tidying up is concerned, but somehow I never seem to be able to keep it up.'

'That's all right,' he responded, deceptively mild. 'I'm always full of good intentions where not yelling at people is concerned—but somehow I never seem to be able to keep that up either.'

CHAPTER SIX

ALTHOUGH the winter sun was bright, it was impossible to forget that it was early January—the fresh breeze blowing in from the sea had a sting like ice. But Lynne didn't mind a bit. Strolling back from the shops two days later, she paused by the harbour wall to breathe in the salt-laden air and watch a battered old lobster boat unloading its catch.

Shopping was not a chore she normally enjoyed—especially routine food shopping. But this morning it had been a pleasure wandering along the narrow streets behind the harbour and through the little covered market that in summer was teeming with tourists but was now half-empty. All the shopkeepers had been ready for a friendly chat, and perfectly happy for her to squeeze the vegetables and haggle over the exact cut of beef she wanted.

It had also been something of a relief to get out of the cottage for a while. She had been planning to make a start on her book today, but she had found that, although she had thought she knew exactly what she wanted to write, once she had settled herself at the dining-room table, with her laptop computer, her portable printer and a neat stack of A4 paper, the words had proved strangely elusive.

She had sat for a while, trying to will herself into a creative frame of mind, that infuriating little cursor flashing on the blank screen as if taunting her lack of productivity. The rapid clicking of the keyboard from the room next door, where Rhys had his desk, had indicated that he was having no such difficulty...

So much for peace and tranquillity, she now reflected wryly—sharing the house with him was not calculated to help her get on with her work at all. Damn him, why did he have to be here, unsettling her, making her start to wish that her dreams could become real? Life would have been so much simpler, so much safer, if he had stayed in her fantasy world, where he belonged.

With a small sigh she picked up her shopping bag and crossed the cobbled street to climb the steep hill back towards the cottage. But as she turned the corner by the Smuggler's Rest, her shoulders hunched slightly against the chilling wind, she almost collided with a tall figure, limping slightly and leaning on a metal hand-crutch.

'What are you doing here?' she protested on a small gasp of surprise. 'The doctor said you were to keep your weight off your leg.'

Those hard grey eyes glittered like polished steel. 'I'm not a cripple,' he retorted, that familiar impatient edge to his voice. 'I came down for my lunch.' He indicated the pub behind her. 'You can join me if you like.'

Lynne hesitated. As an invitation it lacked some degree of enthusiasm, but... After all, she *was* quite hungry—and it was a tiring walk back up the hill. 'I...might as well,' she responded, with a casual shrug of her slender shoulders—her indifference was perhaps a little studied, but she wouldn't want him to think she was too eager to have lunch with him.

The pub was pleasantly cosy. The beams of the ceiling were so low that Rhys had to duck his head beneath them, a fire blazed in a deep hearth, throwing out a welcoming glow of heat, and there was a threadbare old armchair at the end of the bar which seemed to be occupied by the Ancient Mariner's elder brother, cupping a half-pint glass of stout in his gnarled hands as if it were a crock of gold.

The landlord greeted Rhys with a broad grin. 'Well, you stupid sod, what have you done to yourself, then?' he enquired, nodding at the metal crutch.

Rhys laughed, propping himself on a bar stool. 'Nothing too serious—it'll be OK in a day or two. Give me a pint of bitter, please, Bill, and one of your Joyce's steak and kidney pies. And top up old Sam's glass. Lynne, what would you like to drink?'

'Er...I'll have a tomato juice, please, and...I think I'll have a Cornish pasty,' she decided, choosing from the menu chalked roughly on the blackboard behind the bar.

The landlord nodded, leaning back to call the order through a hatch into the kitchen behind him. 'All right,' a woman's voice called back testily. 'I'm doing Sam's shepherd's pie.' A hot face appeared at the hatch, but when she saw Rhys she beamed. 'Ah, now why didn't you say it was for Rhys?' she scolded her husband. 'Plenty of chips, is it? Coming up—just the way you like it.'

'Heard you had quite a night of it on Saturday out by Doom Point,' Bill remarked, sliding a glass beneath one of the traditional pump handles—the real ale fanatics in the newsroom would go crazy if they knew of this place, Lynne reflected with a touch of wry amusement.

'It was pretty rough,' Rhys acknowledged.

'Damned fools—putting out on a night like that.' Bill grunted, deftly tipping the glass to get a perfect creamy head on the beer, and then reaching behind him without needing to look to put his hand on a bottle of tomato juice. 'Don't they ever bother listening to the weather report?' He glanced up as the door opened again and two more customers came in. 'Ain't that right, Curran?' he called across. 'We were just talking about those idiots the other night.'

The lifeboat coxswain couldn't have been mistaken for anything other than a Cornishman; his weather-beaten face was round and ruddy, his hair thick and curly, just turning from black to grizzled grey, and he stood with the solid, balanced stance of a sailor unfamiliar with dry land.

He chuckled as he joined them at the bar. 'Oh, they'll have learned their lesson now, right enough,' he asserted. He slapped Rhys on the back with cheerful camaraderie. 'So, how's the knee?' he demanded. 'No permanent damage, I hope? I need you back on the crew.'

Rhys shook his head. 'A couple of weeks at the outside,' he responded, sipping his beer.

The younger of the two newcomers, a big, broad-faced, smiling lad, was eyeing Lynne with undisguised appreciation. 'I see you've got yourself well looked after, anyway,' he declared, winking broadly at Rhys. 'Aren't you going to introduce us?'

Something about the set of that hard mouth gave Lynne the impression that Rhys would have preferred not to, though she couldn't see why he should refuse. 'Curran, Dennis—this is Lynne,' he said tersely.

The young man smiled at her—in spite of his bravado, there was something endearingly bashful about him. 'Pleased to meet you,' he said. 'Rhys never told us he had his girlfriend coming down to stay.'

'I'm not his girlfriend,' she insisted quickly. 'I'm just. . .his landlady. I own the cottage.'

'Oh?' His manner changed abruptly to one of wary hostility. 'Don't see you down here too often at this time of year, though, do we? Considering you liked the place enough to buy a house here.'

'Shut up, Dennis,' Curran cut in sharply. 'She never bought the place. She's one of old Sholto's nieces—ain't that right, girl?'

'Yes, it is,' she confirmed, smiling with surprise and pleasure. 'Did you know him?'

'Know him? I used to sail with him as a lad—on the mackerel boats. He was a fine seaman—taught me all I know about the tides and currents hereabouts. You'd be his sister Connie's granddaughter. I remember you when you were a little girl, when you used to come down here visiting—you and your sister. You used to sit on the lobster pots on the harbour wall, eating ice creams.'

'Yes, that's right!' she remembered, laughing. 'Goodness, fancy you remembering that!'

'You're old Sholto's family? Well, why didn't you say?' Dennis protested, abandoning both his hostility and his ribaldry. With a gallant flourish he hooked over a barstool for her. 'Here, sit yourself down, lass. You're no foreigner—you're practically kin!'

She laughed, warmed by this unexpected welcome; in all the years she had been coming down here she had never really got to know any of the villagers—certainly not enough to sit chatting like this with them. Of course, it was different in the winter, when there were no tourists—she had often been conscious of an 'us and them' divide, and, while she didn't like it, she could hardly blame the locals for resenting the temporary influx that disrupted their lives each summer—even if many of them did make their living from the trade it brought.

Everyone soon had drinks; neither Curran nor Dennis was drinking alcohol, Lynne noticed—the crew must have to be in a constant state of readiness in case there was a 'shout' for the lifeboat. They all lived and worked within a few minutes' dash to the boat-house—Dennis, she soon learned, worked in his father's garage on the far side of the harbour.

'Trouble with your ignition? You bring it down to me,' he insisted when she mentioned the problems with her car. 'I'll have it fixed it for you in no time.'

'Thank you.' She smiled up at him with friendly warmth, comfortable with his unthreatening flattery—after the emotional strain of being around Rhys it was quite restful. He was in discussion with Curran—something about the boat—but she was conscious of him watching her, a metallic glitter in those hard grey eyes.

She made herself ignore him, chatting instead with Dennis and Bill. The landlord had been on the crew himself, when he was younger, and he had a fund of stories about the boat's history—some of them made her shudder, especially when they talked about an earlier boat which had sunk with the loss of all hands. She slanted a covert glance at Rhys from beneath her lashes, thinking of Saturday night's storm; he had been out in that, and as soon as his knee was better he would be out in one again...

'Of course, the modern boats won't capsize,' Curran assured her, picking up her anxious look. 'With the door sealed, they self-right in seconds. It was in the old days that they were the real heroes—used to go out in little rowboats. And with the fishing fleet they used to have a lot of business. Nowadays we might go six or eight weeks without a shout.'

She wasn't entirely reassured, but she felt that with the bluff Cornish seaman in charge the crew were in the safest hands.

'The trouble these days is getting a full muster,' Curran explained. 'Especially in the winter. There's not much work around, so a lot of the local men have moved away. And it's a lot to ask—being ready to go out at any time, with no pay. We're always glad of the chance to pick up a good volunteer,' he added, with a grin for Rhys. 'Especially one with experience on radar and radio.'

And Rhys, Lynne suspected, was glad of something that would give him the chance of some real action—there was no way he would be content just to sit writing about it, not now he had fully recovered from the injury he had picked up in South America. He just wasn't the type to settle for a quiet life!

The old ship's clock on the wall chimed twice. Curran heaved a sigh, and rose to his feet. 'Well, come on, then, Dennis; let's be getting back. See you, Bill. Cheerio, Lynne—it was nice to meet you. You'll have to bring her down on Sunday,' he added to Rhys, a twinkle in his eyes. 'Any extra pair of hands is welcome when we're giving the old crate a bit of spit and polish.'

Lynne hesitated, flickering an uncertain glance towards Rhys. In spite of her earlier protest, it seemed that people had made their own assumptions about the nature of their relationship. But she felt awkward about denying it again—it would probably only convince them all the more that there was something in it.

'Thank you—I'd like to come and help, if I can,' she responded, managing a smile.

'Good! See you Sunday, then. Cheers!'

'We'll be off too, Bill,' said Rhys, finishing his beer. 'See you tomorrow.'

'Aye. Mind how you go—don't go falling down no more stairs!' the landlord admonished with the kind of chuckle which hinted that it was other, more private physical activities he had in mind.

The wind was still blowing vigorously off the sea as they walked up the hill. Lynne swung her shopping bag as she strode along—Rhys didn't seem to be relying on his hand-crutch very much now, she noted with some relief, so his knee must be getting better.

'Well, that was a nice lunch,' she remarked happily. 'I really enjoyed it.'

He glanced down at her, one level eyebrow lifted in sardonic enquiry. 'Oh? I wouldn't have thought it was quite your usual scene.'

'It isn't,' she conceded, stung. 'But they're nice people down here. Genuine.' Rather different from the fair-weather friends she had left behind in London, she mused—the ones who had been too busy to return her calls after she had been fired from her job.

Rhys made a noise that might have been a snort and walked on, leaving Lynne glaring after him in seething fury. If he was going to be like that, he could just move out of her cottage! And she'd tell him so...as soon as they got home.

'Well, this is a flying start.' Lynne sighed, dropping her chin onto her cupped hand and staring despondently at the three limp sentences which were all she had managed in as many hours. She hadn't expected it to be easy, but this was ridiculous! 'Oh, dammit!'

Impatiently she rose to her feet and picked up the coffee-mug she had only just emptied. In the next room, Rhys was working steadily. And he wouldn't appreciate being disturbed, she warned herself—even as she called out to ask him if he wanted another cup of coffee.

The response took several seconds—seconds that eloquently conveyed his irritation at the interruption, as did his terse, 'Thank you.'

She pulled a face and went through to the kitchen.

There hadn't been a suitable opportunity this afternoon to bring up the issue of his moving out. As soon as they had got back from the pub, he had sat down to work again, with a self-discipline she could only admire. Maybe there was some kind of trick to it—she ought to ask him. . .

She glanced up quickly as he strolled into the kitchen. 'Oh. . .hi. I hope I didn't disturb you,' she remarked, wishing her heart wouldn't thump like that whenever he was around.

That hard mouth curved into a faintly grim smile. 'It was time to take a break,' he responded lazily.

'How's it going?' she asked brightly, focusing all her attention on filling the kettle.

'Not bad.'

'Where's this one set?'

'Libya.'

'Oh. That. . .sounds interesting.' She washed out the mugs, wiping them quickly dry on the teatowel, and reached up to the cupboard for the jar of coffee. If only he wouldn't sit there watching her like that, those grey eyes inscrutable. It made her nervous. . .

'How are you getting on?' he enquired with polite interest.

She shrugged with casual nonchalance. 'Oh. . .not bad.' *Ask his advice*, a small voice prompted her. But she hadn't even told Carole what she was trying to do; until she had had some success, she didn't want anyone to know—least of all R.J. Hunter, who could currently earn a million-dollar advance for merely addressing an envelope.

'What is it you're working on?'

'Oh, it's just an article—for a magazine,' she lied defensively.

'What about?'

'About...women. Career women.' He knew she didn't want to tell him—she could tell from that metallic glint of suspicion in his eyes.

'Can I see it?' he enquired, in that deceptively soft voice that somehow, without any overt hint of threat, managed to convey the warning that it would be better for her if she answered his questions.

'Er...when it's finished. It's...a rather long article. In fact it's a series of articles.' Even to her own ears, her voice sounded unconvincing.

'I see.' There was a perceptible hardness in his tone. *Idiot*, she castigated herself crossly—all she had succeeded in doing was reinforcing his suspicion that she was writing about him.

The kettle was boiling and she quickly turned it off. The lid of the coffee jar was tight, and she had to struggle to unscrew it—and as it came loose the coffee spilled all over the floor. 'Oh, dammit...' She grabbed the first thing that came to her hand, which happened to be the teatowel, and stooped to mop up the mess she had made.

'Are you always such a disaster in the kitchen?' Rhys enquired drily.

'I'm just not the domestic type,' she responded, her temper jagged. Not that she was usually so clumsy—it was only when he was around...

With a small sigh of exasperation he went over to a cupboard and brought out the dustpan and brush, crouching beside her to sweep up the coffee-grounds deftly and throw them in the bin. Then he got a piece of kitchen paper, dampened it, and wiped up the last of the residue, leaving the floor clean.

'Thank you...' she murmured as he straightened beside her.

'It's a good job you were never in the Army,' he remarked, an unexpected glint of humour in those hard grey eyes.

Gazing up at him, she felt her heart kick sharply against her ribs. 'I'd probably have spent most of my time in the glasshouse for insubordination in the ranks,' she responded, trying for a casual tone.

He laughed, low and huskily, taking a step towards her so that she was trapped against the big stone sink—and as she leaned back, gasping at the unexpected move, he smiled down at her with sardonic humour. 'I suspect insubordination would have been the least of the Army's problems,' he murmured with lazy mockery. 'I'm afraid you'd have been a serious distraction for the troops.'

His hands slid around her slender waist, curving her towards him, and as his head bent over her she knew that this time, at last, he was going to kiss her for real.

His mouth was warm and enticing, coaxing her lips apart to admit the languorous invasion of his tongue, swirling over all the sweet, secret membranes within. Hesitantly she began to respond; there was such a difference in their heights that she was having to tip her head back until she felt dizzy, and she had to put up her hands against the hard wall of his chest to steady herself—encountering the firm resilience of male muscle beneath the soft cotton-jersey sweater he was wearing. It was just the way it had been in her dreams...

But this was no dream—he was far too real and solid, his arms strong around her, his kiss deeper and more demanding as she yielded all her defences. She knew she shouldn't be letting this happen, but right now her mind couldn't focus on the reasons why—not with that subtle, musky male scent drugging her mind, tempting her to surrender to the aching temptation.

She could only close her eyes, losing herself in a tide

of sweet, honeyed warmth that was filling her veins as she melted against him, her body curved intimately close against the hard length of his. His tongue was swirling in a flagrantly sensual exploration, deep into her mouth, ravaging her senses, igniting fires that were flaming swiftly out of control.

But a niggling little voice inside her head was taunting her with warnings. This *wasn't* a dream—this was real life. In her dreams there had been no question that he had been wildly, wonderfully in love with her, but in real life he didn't even seem to like her very much. But then, a man didn't need to like a woman in order to make love to her, she reminded herself tartly—it was simply a matter of satisfying his physical needs.

He must know that she was powerfully attracted to him—she hadn't been too successful at disguising that fact—and he had every reason to assume that she would have a pretty liberal attitude to sex—he knew the kind of sophisticated media circles she'd moved in, knew that she had apparently been happy to live with Paul without the benefit of a wedding ring. Why should he doubt that she would be willing to indulge in a casual relationship with him—strictly no strings attached?

But appearances could be deceptive. She *wasn't* the kind of woman who could skip lightly into bed with any man who happened to take her fancy; she had really believed herself to be in love with Paul, had desperately wanted to marry him—and she'd thought that he had felt the same. Only she had been wrong.

With the memory of that betrayal, some semblance of pride began to reassert itself, and she forced herself to draw back from him, dragging in a long, deep breath to steady herself before pinning a brittle smile in place. 'Coffee,' she asserted firmly. 'I'm afraid I don't have time for anything else—I have work to do.'

His laughter was cool and mocking. 'Ah, yes—work. Pardon me for forgetting—you're a career woman, aren't you? If you'll excuse my use of the sexist term. Work before pleasure—isn't that it?'

'Y-yes it is,' she confirmed, unable to keep her voice quite steady when he was looking at her with that mesmeric gaze.

'What was it you said you were working on, by the way?' The question was almost casually put, but there was no mistaking the hard intent that lay beneath it.

To her chagrin, Lynne felt her cheeks tinge with a blush of embarrassment that might so easily be mistaken for guilt. 'I told you. It's...a series of articles.'

'When's your deadline?'

'Er...in a few weeks.'

'Who are they for?' he enquired, picking at her deceit in a way that was quite unnerving.

'A women's magazine,' she managed. 'You wouldn't have heard of it.'

'Oh, I might.' His voice was as smooth and treacherous as black ice. 'Helena used to read those things by the bale.'

'It's a new one,' she asserted, her lies getting a little desperate. 'It's not been published yet.'

'What's it going to be called?'

'They haven't settled on a name.'

'I see.'

'I'm telling you the truth,' she insisted raggedly. 'I wouldn't write about you without your agreement.'

'That's very reassuring,' he countered, chilling her with his icy gaze. 'I just can't help wondering how far you'd be willing to go to try to persuade me.'

Sunday was a beautiful clear, bright, winter's day—cold but invigorating. The boatshed was a hive of purposeful activity: most of the eleven-strong crew were there, many of them with their families, checking equipment, polishing brasses, scrubbing down the deck. Their pride in the sleek boat, with its dark blue steel hull and vivid orange cabin, was obvious.

Lynne had been inside the boatshed before, as a

visitor on open days in the summer, peeking around it in return for a donation, but that wasn't the same as feeling like part of the team. And she did—she had never been made to feel more welcome anywhere. Her old uncle, who, to her as a child, had seemed doddery and slow, had clearly been held in much respect locally, and her relationship to him had proved a passport to acceptance in a county where anyone who hailed from beyond the Tamar still tended to be regarded as a foreigner.

Rhys's passport, she quickly recognised, had been his willingness to put his skills at the disposal of the lifeboat crew. Though he deferred to Curran, who as coxswain was in overall charge of the boat, it was clear that the corner of the cabin which held the radar, aquasounder and radio was chiefly his responsibility.

He was now more or less fully mobile again, but nothing had been said by either of them about his moving out of the cottage. There had been no repetition of the incident by the kitchen sink either, though they both seemed a little...guarded with each other, a little too polite—a little wary, perhaps, of getting too close.

She had been anxious that people would jump to the wrong conclusion about the fact that she and Rhys were living in the same house, afraid that she would meet with some disapproval, but, though it seemed that people *had* made the obvious assumption, it didn't seem to be causing any problems.

'That's a great job you're doing there, lass,' Curran said approvingly, strolling past as she paused to admire the gleam that her energetic efforts were producing on the windows along the side of the cabin. 'Keep it up—there's five more down t'other side!'

She laughed, breathing on the glass to rub away a greasy mark—and laughed again as Dennis popped his head up inside the window and pulled a face at her.

'That's what I like to see,' he declared, swinging round the door. 'I love work—I could stand around and watch it for hours.' Since he had been busy in the engine-hatch all morning, Lynne knew that she could safely take this remark with a pinch of salt. 'You didn't bring that car of yours down for me to take a look at,' he added on a note of gentle reproof.

'No—but I will. Thank you, Dennis,' she responded, smiling.

'No trouble,' he assured her. 'I just thought...maybe...' He slanted a swift glance up towards where Rhys stood, all his attention on the radar antenna on the roof of the cabin. 'If it was right, what you said the other day—about just being his landlady, and all—well, I wondered if maybe we might go out for a drink or something one evening, you and me? Only...I wouldn't ask if I thought you and he were...you know...'

Lynne shook her head, her soft mouth curved into a wry smile. 'We're not,' she affirmed, feeling a little awkward. 'But...even so...I'd rather that we were just friends, Dennis.'

A shadow of disappointment crossed his wide, honest face, but then he grinned. 'All right,' he conceded. 'I had a feeling you'd say that, but I thought it would do no harm asking, eh?'

'No harm at all,' she agreed readily, relieved that he had taken it so well.

'You bring your car down anyway, though,' he insisted. 'You don't want it conking out on you—not down here, where you could be miles from anywhere.'

'Thanks, Dennis—I will.'

'Will what?' They both glanced up, startled, as Rhys appeared above them on the cabin roof. As he slid down onto the deck Dennis mumbled something apologetic and faded quickly away. 'What was that all about?' Rhys demanded, as if he had an absolute right to know.

Lynne sighed with weary impatience—if he was going to take that kind of attitude, it was little wonder that Dennis didn't believe her denials that there was anything between them. 'I was just saying I'd take my car down for him to have a look at the ignition,' she explained with cool dignity.

'I hope you're not leading him on,' Rhys grated, those hard eyes flecked with anger.

'Leading him on? What on earth do you mean?' she protested, taken aback.

'You know what I mean.'

He stepped past her, swinging himself down the ladder to the boathouse floor. Lynne stared after him, puzzled, confused—and finally exasperated. Did he really think that she was so shallow and self-centred as to play hurtful games with someone as open and unsophisticated as the young mechanic?

Well, damn him—she didn't care what he thought. She had as much right to be here, to make friends with these people, as he did. And if he didn't like it he could just find himself somewhere else to stay while he finished his stupid book—it was her cottage, after all.

In fact she really ought to have told him to leave already, she reminded herself firmly—though he had made no attempt to step across the invisible line she had drawn between them since Tuesday, there was no certainty that he wouldn't give it another try. It might even seem as if she were tacitly encouraging him by letting him stay. So she would tell him that she wanted him to go—she would do it this afternoon, as soon as they got home.

After a busy morning's work most of the crew adjourned for a roistering—though strictly non-alcoholic—lunch in the Smuggler's Rest on the harbour, so it was the middle of the afternoon by the time they strolled up the hill to the cottage. It had turned cold, an icy wind slicing in from the sea, but as Lynne opened the door of the cottage the warmth from the Aga welcomed them home.

Her sigh of contentment turned to a yawn as she shrugged off her jacket. 'Ah...goodness, I'm tired! It must be all that fresh air and hard work.'

Those hard dark eyes slanted her a look of sardonic question. 'Work? From what I could see, you were spending most of your time flirting with Dennis.'

'I was not!' she protested, indignant. 'I was just being friendly.'

'So you've got him to look at your car for you. Well done.'

'He offered!' she retorted hotly. 'And besides, I'll be paying him—I wasn't expecting him to do it for free. Anyway, it's none of your business,' she snapped, turning sharply away from him.

'Oh, yes, it is.' He caught her shoulder, swinging her around and into his arms. 'He's one of the lifeboat crew, and he needs to have his mind on his job, not mooning after you. If you want someone to play around with, you'd better make do with me.'

He pulled her against the hard length of his body, and as her lips parted on a small gasp of shock his mouth captured hers, hot and insistent, his tongue ravaging the sweet, moist recesses within in a flagrantly sensual exploration that had her struggling against an overwhelming tide of response—wanting to be angry at the way he was treating her but unable to resist the deep, female urge to surrender to his fierce demand.

Surrender won. She was melting helplessly against him, her body curved intimately against his as his hands slid slowly down the length of her spine. Her mind was spinning in a vortex of confusion, unable to grasp at any rational thought—only some crazy one about still waters running much deeper than she had expected, after all.

He was arousing her with an expertise against which she could have no defence, his languorous tongue searching out all the most sensitive corners of her mouth, his hand lifting to cup and caress her small, firm breasts through the thick layer of her cable-knit sweater. She was breathing raggedly, her head tipping back and then falling against his shoulder as she gasped for air, and then he trailed a path of scalding kisses down the long, vulnerable column of her throat, before tilting her head back up again, to reclaim her mouth with a ruthless tenderness that fuelled the aching longing inside her—a longing that she was forced to acknowledge had been growing steadily from the very first time she had met him.

She knew that she ought to be stopping him, but she didn't know how. Maybe it had been like this with Paul in the early days—surely it must have been? But it had been too long since she had felt like this, and she didn't want it to end. Ever. Even though she knew that yielding to this sweet temptation would exact a high price. He had accused her of playing around, but he was the one to whom this was nothing but a game.

Somehow—she wasn't quite sure how they had got there—she found herself tipping backwards onto the sofa, half-pinned beneath his weight. With a swift movement he had pulled her sweater off over her head, dragging her T-shirt with it, to find that beneath it she was wearing only the skimpiest lacy scrap of a bra.

She drew in a long, ragged breath, a shiver of nervous apprehension tingling down her spine as she watched his eyes, watched him smile in slow satisfaction as his hot gaze surveyed her slender body, lingering over the swell of her small breasts cupped in the delicate white lace.

'Very pretty,' he murmured smokily, the tip of one finger tracing the edge of the lace against her skin until he found the clip that fastened it at the front, nestling in the soft shadow between her breasts. 'Very pretty indeed.'

She closed her eyes, a soft sigh escaping her lips as he deftly unfastened it and brushed it aside to uncover the warm, naked roundness, pertly tipped with pink. A honeyed warmth flowed through her as he caressed her, his touch smooth and firm against her silken skin, circling lazily over the aching swell, until at last he took the tender nubs lightly between his fingers, teasing them into a state of the most exquisite arousal.

'Please...' she whispered on a ragged sob.

He laughed softly. 'Is that "please stop" or "please go on"?'

Stop! some last shred of sanity warned her urgently. But those treacherous longings inside her refused to listen. 'Please...go on,' she begged helplessly.

'That's what I thought you meant.'

Her breathing was shallow, impeded, and she heard herself moaning softly as he bent his head over the vulnerable curve of her naked breasts, swirling his hot tongue around the dainty pink nipples, nipping at them with his hard white teeth, tormenting her with pleasure. And then he drew one sizzlingly sensitised peak into his mouth, suckling at it with a deep, hungry rhythm, until her spine was arching in ecstasy, her head dizzy from the fevered swirl of her blood.

'So,' he murmured, lifting his head to survey her state of half-naked abandon. 'Are you still tired?'

She opened her eyes, shaking her head as she gazed up at him in bewilderment.

That hard mouth had curved into a sardonic smile. 'But would you like to go to bed anyway?' he queried tauntingly.

She hesitated, struggling to find the will to refuse him—she knew only too well that he would be taking her purely to satisfy some transient physical need. But that was as much as she could hope for—only in her dreams could there ever be more. And the temptation to surrender, to know how it would feel to have him caress her naked body, to have him lie above her as he had that day by the riverbank, but this time to yield to the full demand of his hard penetration, was more than she could withstand.

'Yes...'

He laughed in lazy triumph, and, rising to his feet, scooped her up in his arms as if she weighed nothing at all and strode towards the stairs. She wrapped her arms around his neck, breathing in the evocative, musky scent of his skin, lost to any thought of the consequences of what she was about to do.

The sharp ring of the doorbell startled them both. 'Damn!' he muttered, pausing only briefly and then deciding to ignore it. 'They'll go away in a minute.'

But Lynne had been brought abruptly to her senses, and to her the interruption seemed like fate giving her one last chance—if she let it pass, she would only have herself to blame when her heart was broken beyond repair. 'No—it...might be important,' she protested, struggling in his arms. 'We ought to see who it is.'

Those hard grey eyes flared with heat, but he set her down on her feet. 'If you insist,' he grated, impatience slicing his voice. 'Go and answer it.'

Scampering quickly across the room, she grabbed for her T-shirt and pulled it on, tucking her bra out of sight in a corner of the sofa, beneath her discarded sweater. And then, drawing in a long, steadying breath, she made herself walk calmly across to front door and open it.

The icy bite of the wind caught her, but it wasn't that which struck like a knife into her heart. The woman on the doorstep was beautiful—one of those effortlessly elegant blondes who looked as if her family owned half of Gloucestershire. She wore a flatteringly cut camel-hair coat, set off with a clever twist of silk scarf at her throat, and her hair was drawn back into a loose chignon—not a hair of it out of place, even in this wind. And her earrings were real pearls set in gold.

The other woman recovered quickly from her surprise, her cool glance taking in the evidence of the cosy cottage and Lynne's flustered state, and then she smiled with tolerant understanding. 'I'm sorry—I didn't realise Rhys had anyone down here with him.' Her voice was low and well modulated, as polished as her appearance. 'May I come in? I'm his wife.'

CHAPTER SEVEN

'*Ex*-WIFE.' Rhys's voice had an edge like a new razor-blade, and Lynne glanced at him in surprise.

The other woman did not seem at all daunted by this unpromising welcome. She laughed chidingly, shaking her head. 'Not quite ex,' she corrected him in a tone of mild reproof.

He lifted one level eyebrow in sardonic query. 'Pardon me? I thought we got a divorce? Maybe my memory's not what it used to be.'

His wife smiled, clearly accustomed to this kind of temper. 'We got a decree nisi—or rather, you did. But it isn't final yet.'

'It is as far as I'm concerned.' He sat down in one of the armchairs, his air of cool indifference belied by the tension Lynne could sense in every line of his body. 'It's only you that's dragging it out.'

He hadn't invited his wife to take a seat, but she sat down anyway, perfectly composed, her back straight and her legs neatly crossed at the ankle and tucked to one side. Lynne had closed the front door but remained hovering uncertainly in the background, fervently wishing she could be anywhere else but here—the last thing she wanted was to witness this scene, but it would be no less awkward if she tried to slip away.

And in her faded T-shirt and jeans, grubby from working on the lifeboat, she felt at a distinct disadvantage—Rhys's wife was so stylishly elegant that she would have made anyone else look like a frump. And if she can't hold him, what chance have I got? she mused bitterly. It was fortunate that the bell had rung when it had—going to bed with him would have been the biggest mistake of her life.

'Darling, I do understand the way you feel.' That

voice was soft and refined, effortlessly charming. 'You've been through a difficult time. And I admit there were faults on both sides...' Rhys's contemptuous snort graphically emphasised his opinion of that comment, but his wife smilingly passed over it. 'I'm trying to say I don't blame you for...whatever.' She slanted another of those sweetly understanding smiles towards Lynne. 'These things happen.'

Lynne felt her cheeks flame scarlet. With those few words she had been effectively dismissed as a minor peccadillo, a casual fling, a temporary bit on the side—which was a role she had been all too willing to accept, she was forced to acknowledge.

Rhys appeared to be amused by the whole situation. 'Ah—I haven't introduced you, have I? Lynne—Helena; Helena—Lynne. Lynne's my...er...landlady,' he added, doing absolutely nothing to correct his wife's obvious assumption. 'She owns this cottage.'

'Really?' Helena Gillam-Fox glanced around the comfortable sitting room, her cultured eye assessing the taste and deciding it wasn't quite for her. 'It's charming, my dear—quite charming.' The honey in the woman's voice was beginning to get a little sticky.

'Thank you.'

'So, what are you doing here?' Rhys asked of his wife, his tone one of bored lack of interest. 'It's a long way to come down from London merely for a social call.'

'I would have telephoned,' she responded, smiling again, 'but it's so difficult to get you to hold a civilised conversation without putting the phone down. Besides, I've only come from Bath. I'm staying with your father for a few days. He does get lonely, you know—someone has to keep him company.'

'How noble of you.'

His wife ignored the jibe. 'And it's his birthday on Friday. He'll be seventy, in case you've forgotten. I thought it would be nice to arrange a little dinner party for him—nothing too elaborate, just a few very close friends. Even Simon has managed to arrange to take a few days to come down with Fiona, but naturally it wouldn't seem right without you there.'

Lynne could see the metallic glitter in Rhys's narrowed eyes. 'Really? I don't see why. We usually manage to rub each other up the wrong way.'

She laughed merrily, as if he had made some kind of joke. 'Oh, don't be silly! You *are* his eldest son, after all.'

'That doesn't mean I have to sit down and have dinner with him.'

'But it's his birthday!' she protested, clearly shocked by his attitude. 'And, after all, at his age... Well, not to put too fine a point on it, he may not have many more.'

'Don't be melodramatic,' Rhys returned drily. 'He'll almost certainly outlive all of us.'

For a moment Lynne thought that the air of inviolable calm was going to waver, but Helena Gillam-Fox was far too self-possessed to allow herself to be needled so easily. 'I'm sure we all *hope* so,' she purred in that soft, sweet, resolute voice. 'But you can never be *completely* sure, can you? And if—heaven forbid!— anything *should* happen to him, you will at least have made your peace with him.'

Rhys stretched his arms above his head, yawning, weary of the conversation. 'I'll deal with that problem if it ever arises,' he drawled lazily. 'And as for this cosy little birthday party—count me out.'

Helena sighed, shaking her head sadly, and then glanced up appealingly at Lynne. 'Won't *you* try to persuade him?'

'Me?' She blinked at her in astonishment. 'I...I really don't think...'

'To be honest, I arranged the whole thing in the hope that Rhys would agree to come,' Helena confessed wryly. 'The Brigadier will be so disappointed if you aren't there, darling. I know he finds it very difficult to show it, but he really is very fond of you. It can't have been easy for him, being left with the two of you when your mother died—you and Simon are all he's got left now.'

He slanted her a look of cold steel. 'You really know how to put the knife in and twist it, don't you—*darling*?' he countered acidly. 'All right, she's persuaded us, hasn't she, Lynne? We'll come.'

'We...?' Lynne stared at him, startled.

'*We...?*' It had clearly not occurred to his wife, either, that such might be his response.

His hard mouth curved into a humourless smile—a warning of trouble. 'Of course. That's not a problem, is it?'

Helena flushed slightly, but her control was superior to Lynne's. 'Of course not,' she responded in that sad, sweet, dignified voice before Lynne could choke out a word. 'I told you, darling, I quite understand...how things are. Although I'm...sure you know it doesn't have to be that way. It isn't too late, even now.'

Rhys laughed without humour, leaning back in the armchair and closing his eyes. 'It was too late for us even before we got married, Helena,' he sighed. 'I was never going to be who you wanted me to be. You've got what you came for—so, goodbye.'

She hesitated, but then smiled wryly, shaking her head. 'Very well, I'm going,' she conceded, rising gracefully to her feet. 'I'll see you on Friday. Don't forget—you promised.' She turned to Lynne, her smile taut. 'I hope you'll make sure he comes.'

'I'm...not sure that I can...'

'We'll come,' Rhys confirmed, his voice sleek and treacherous. 'Goodbye, Helena.'

She sighed and shrugged her slim shoulders. 'Goodbye, Rhys.' He didn't move or open his eyes as she walked to the door. She glanced back a little uncertainly, as if she wanted to say something else, then seemed to realise she would be wasting her breath; so, with another wry, faintly apologetic smile for Lynne, she turned away, letting herself out and closing the door behind her.

There was a long, uncomfortable silence. Rhys remained where he was, his eyes closed, his expression unreadable; Lynne made her escape to the kitchen, her thoughts and emotions tangled into knots. Outside she heard Helena's car start up and drive away, its sound fading as it turned the corner and headed down through the village.

One thing was obvious at least, she reflected with a bitter twist of pain. In spite of what he had said, his marriage was not yet over—either legally or emotionally. The mere fact that he had been so abrupt and hostile towards his wife demonstrated that his feelings for her were still unresolved—if that weren't so, he wouldn't have been so bothered by her visit.

So once again, it seemed, she had got herself mixed up with a man in the throes of a messy divorce. *Fool*, she castigated herself angrily. Don't you ever learn? She had known, of course, that he could never be for her, but meeting his ex-wife had cruelly reinforced that fact. The image of that lovely face, fine-boned and refined, lingered like the hint of subtle, expensive perfume she had left behind. If she was lucky, she could perhaps hold his interest for a little while—but she could never step into Helena's elegant shoes.

Rhys appeared in the doorway, leaning one wide shoulder against the frame, a cold glitter in his eyes. 'Well?' he demanded, a hard edge to his voice. 'Aren't you going to say anything?'

'What do you expect me to say?' she countered defensively. 'You weren't very nice to her. At least you could have offered her a cup of coffee—it's a long drive from Bath.'

He laughed with dry humour. 'Oh, don't worry about Helena—she's got the hide of a rhinoceros.'

'You...didn't tell me you were still married,' she remarked, picking up a dishcloth and wiping down the draining board, although it was already spotless.

'I'm not, to all intents and purposes,' he responded with cool indifference. 'The decree becomes final in a couple of weeks, and there's nothing Helena can do to prevent it. I don't know why she bothered coming—but then she never did know when she was wasting her time.'

'Maybe she's still in love with you,' Lynne suggested, her heart aching.

He shrugged in a gesture of casual dismissal. 'She was never in love with me—she was in love with what she thought she could make of me,' he asserted grimly. 'At one time she wanted me to go into politics—she had a fancy to be the wife of the Prime Minister. Now she thinks it would be nice to preside over literary soirées—of course I'd have to stop "wasting my talent" on thrillers and write something of serious literary merit.

'The trouble with Helena is that she doesn't like having to let go of anything once she's got her claws into it. That's why she's dreamed up this damned birthday party—it's just another of her little stratagems. It put her nose out of joint a bit, you being here, but she'll have rallied soon enough. This is her last chance to persuade me not to finalise the divorce. She'll be wearing some fabulously elegant creation; and she'll pour her charm over me all night, just to make me realise what a wonderful woman I've let slip through my fingers. You wait—you'll see exactly what I mean.'

Lynne drew in a long, steadying breath. 'I'm not going. You're not using me in your little marital games.'

'Fine,' he countered, unconcerned. 'Then I don't go.'

'But you have to go,' she protested hotly. 'He's your father.'

Those cool grey eyes regarded her with mocking humour. 'You're beginning to sound just like her,' he returned, a sardonic inflection in his voice. 'You weren't taken in by that little performance, were you? Number one, my father has never celebrated a birthday in his life—he barely even acknowledges that he has them. Number two, I don't need to wait for his birthday to "make my peace" with him, as Helena so affectingly put it. We may not manage to agree on a single subject, but I visit him every couple of weeks. And the last time I saw him—which was two weeks ago—he was in the most robust of health and thoroughly relishing a forthcoming confrontation with the Department of the Environment, who have the temerity to wish to create a bypass half a mile from the village.'

Lynne hesitated, not quite so certain. 'But even so... If he *is* having a party, and he's expecting you to be there...you can't let him down.'

'I'm not going without protection,' he insisted obdurately. 'I'd rather face a whole line of Iraqi tanks than that woman when she's got her mind set on something. So, if you're so concerned that I should go, you'll have to come with me.'

'That's blackmail!' she protested, her eyes sparking.

'Call it what you like,' he responded lazily. That hard mouth curved into a sardonic smile. 'You've no need to be jealous of her, you know.'

To her chagrin, she felt a heated blush rise to her cheeks. 'Don't be ridiculous,' she protested, her voice catching in her throat. 'Why should I be jealous of your wife?'

'*Ex*-wife. And you are,' he asserted, the knowing glint in his eyes mocking her fragile defences. 'I saw the way you were looking at her—it was written all over your face.'

'You're...imagining things,' she countered, struggling to maintain some semblance of composure. And if she went on rubbing at this draining-board like this she'd rub it away.

'Am I?' The challenge was silky smooth. 'Then why are you afraid to come to this damned birthday party with me?'

Lynne returned him a frosty glare. She should have known that it was impossible to out-manoeuvre such a master tactician, she acknowledged acidly—if she kept on refusing, it would betray the fact that she *was* jealous of Helena. Deeply jealous.

Helena Gillam-Fox was everything that she wasn't—serene, sophisticated, self-assured... She couldn't imagine *her* ever having a fight with him on the stairs and ending up in an undignified heap on the floor! She was exactly the sort of woman who looked as if she belonged at his side.

And, in spite of his present bitterness, he must have been in love with her once to have married her, she mused wistfully. What had gone wrong? She was so beautiful—it was difficult to imagine why any man would leave a wife like that. Unless, of course, he really *wasn't* the marrying kind.

Which was what she had already suspected, she reminded herself a little ruefully. Turning her back on him, she surreptitiously brushed her hand across her eyes—the last thing she wanted was to let him see the tears that were standing in them. He already knew how vulnerable she was, and she had little doubt that he wouldn't hesitate to exploit it. A man would take whatever a woman was stupid enough to give—even a cool, self-contained man like Rhys Gillam-Fox. *Especially* a cool, self-contained man like Rhys Gillam-Fox.

'Anyway, I'm not going to discuss it now,' she declared briskly, rinsing out the dishcloth and hanging it carefully to dry. 'I have work to do this evening.'

He laughed with biting mockery. 'It wasn't work you were thinking about before we were so inconveniently interrupted,' he taunted softly. 'Is that how it was with your fiancé? Always work—never any time to make love?'

He was blocking her way out of the kitchen—deliberately. Someone like Helena would no doubt know exactly how to move a man out of her way with just one look of frosty disdain, but Lynne had never been much good at that sort of thing—she lacked the inches to carry it off. Instead she hesitated, awkward, evading his eyes, her heart starting to beat a little too fast.

He laughed again, sensing her agitation. 'He shouldn't have let you get away with it,' he murmured huskily. He reached out one hand and slid it along the line of her jaw, then round to cage her skull, drawing her inexorably towards him. 'He should have tried a little...persuasion...'

Conflicting emotions were warring in her, the temptation to surrender to the aching physical need inside her fighting with her hurt pride. She was still trying to resolve the dilemma when his mouth came down to brush lightly over hers, sweetly coaxing her lips apart.

She hesitated, struggling to resist, though the musky, male scent of his skin was drugging her senses, stirring responses that were beyond the reach of reason. She closed her eyes, putting her hands up against the hard wall of his chest to hold him away, her spine quivering as the turmoil of uncertainty racked her slender body. His tongue was tracing a lazy path over the sensitive inner membranes of her lips, deliberately seeking to arouse her, and she knew that she was losing the fight...

In spite of everything, she was starting to fall in love with him for real—not just in her dreams. But she didn't want to—she knew there could never be any future in it. And to let him make love to her, to let all those crazy dreams she had indulged in so foolishly over the past many months begin to spill over into reality would make it so much harder to keep her wayward heart under control.

Finding some last desperate instinct for self-preservation, she managed to push herself away from him. 'Look, I told you—I came down here to work,' she asserted, struggling to hold the line of her defences. 'I don't have the time to get involved in some kind of casual sexual relationship with you.'

He shook his head chidingly, the glint in those hard grey eyes taunting her. 'You can't work all the time, you know. Everyone needs a little relaxation now and then—a little...pleasure...'

The husky, sensual note in his voice stroked down over her skin as if he were touching her, and it took every ounce of will-power she possessed to resist the treacherous longings that were tearing her apart. She drew a deep breath, tilting up her chin in haughty disdain.

'Maybe,' she conceded tautly. 'But I have no intention of going to bed with you, and that's the end of the matter.' And, brushing past him, she hurried up the stairs.

Lynne sat on the end of her bed, gazing into the open wardrobe in wry dismay. She didn't have a thing to wear—at least, nothing suitable to compete with the intimidatingly well-dressed Helena Gillam-Fox. She didn't go in much for dresses anyway, and the couple of decent ones she had were at this moment packed in an old trunk, three hundred or so miles away, at her parents' house in Manchester.

She was still thinking over the problem when the telephone rang. Rhys was out, and she hadn't heard the maroons that signalled a 'shout' for the lifeboat, but she hurried quickly downstairs to answer it, just in case.

'Lynne...?' Carole's voice sounded wary, uncertain. 'Hi. Er...it's me. How are you?'

Lynne drew in a long, deep breath and sat down on the bottom stair, the phone in her lap. 'I'm fine,' she responded, her voice very controlled. 'How are you? Did you have a good trip?'

Carole laughed nervously. 'Fabulous, thanks. The weather was absolutely glorious—it seems such a pity to have to come home to freezing cold London. Anyway, I... I rang Mum this afternoon, and she told me you'd gone down to the cottage.'

'That's right,' Lynne responded in tones of sweet sarcasm. 'And what a surprise I got when I arrived.'

'Oh, Lynne, I'm so sorry. I had no idea you were planning to go down there—if I'd known, I'd have told you he was there. But...well, I had a feeling you wouldn't be too keen.'

'Astute of you.'

'He just needed somewhere quiet for a while, to work on his book, and the cottage seemed so perfect,' Carole argued persuasively. 'It was only until Easter—neither of us ever uses it before then anyway. Er...you don't happen to know where he's staying now, do you? He hasn't left a forwarding address for David.'

'He's...still here,' Lynne responded carefully—she really had meant to tell him to leave, but somehow she hadn't quite got round to it.

'Still there? Oh...' Lynne could almost hear her sister's brain ticking over. 'That's nice. So you've...made it up, then?'

'Not exactly. And before you get any ideas, his wife came down to visit yesterday.'

'His *wife*?' Carole exclaimed, startled. 'Good heavens! She's not staying at the cottage, is she?'

'No, she isn't.' Lynne laughed at the image of the *ménage à trois* that the suggestion conjured up. 'Apparently she's staying with his father, somewhere near Bath. As a matter of fact we've been invited over to dinner on Friday,' she added, her voice taut. 'It's his father's birthday.'

'Oh... That should be...fun...'

'Have you ever met her?' Lynne countered drily.

'No, but David has. He said she's...rather striking,' Carole admitted with some reluctance.

'That's probably not a bad description,' Lynne acknowledged. 'And apparently she doesn't want the divorce to go through—she's campaigning to get him back.'

'I don't think there's much chance of that,' Carole mused. 'I don't know exactly why they split, but I gather that it was pretty final. What are you going to wear?'

'I was thinking of Chanel No 5 and a bright smile,' Lynne responded on a note of sardonic resignation. 'With her around, it's likely to be the only way I'll get noticed.'

Carole laughed. 'Don't be daft! No, seriously—you can look really nice when you make the effort.'

'I don't have anything suitable down here,' Lynne admitted, her mouth twisting into a wry grimace; 'nice' wasn't exactly the image she wanted anyway. 'I'd have worn my standard little black frock, but I sent all that stuff home—I didn't think I was going to need it.'

'Hmm.' There was that ominous ticking of Carole's fertile brain again. 'Don't worry about it—leave it to me,' she declared. 'I'll send you something down.'

'Oh, no—don't go to all that trouble,' Lynne protested, taken aback. 'It's not worth it.'

'Oh, yes, it is,' Carole insisted. 'Take it as my way of saying sorry for not asking you about lending Rhys the cottage.'

'Well. . .nothing too over the top, then,' Lynne conceded warily. 'Otherwise I'll go in my yellow summer cotton.'

'Don't do that,' Carole pleaded. 'Don't worry—it'll be great. Trust me—I know what I'm doing!'

She certainly did, Lynne was forced to admit as she regarded her own reflection in the mirror. The box had arrived, as promised, by parcel post, two days after her telephone conversation with Carole, and she had opened it with some trepidation—though she would never deny that her sister had excellent taste, she had been afraid the dress she would choose would be too glamorous for her to feel comfortable.

But it wasn't a dress—it was a trouser-suit in smooth black silk baratheta, cut on the lines of a man's formal dinner suit but just a little more curvaceous, to flatter her slender shape. She had been a little puzzled at first to find that there was no shirt with it—although there was a satin bow-tie, of a vivid shade of sapphire-blue almost the same colour as her eyes—but then she had realised. It wasn't supposed to be worn with a shirt.

The effect was startlingly sexy: the beautifully tailored jacket subtly skimmed her soft feminine curves, and the saucy bow-tie provocatively underlined the 'naked underneath' look, drawing irresistible attention to the soft hint of shadow defining the contours of her breasts. It certainly wasn't the sort of thing that Helena would ever wear—which was perhaps the best thing in its favour. As she couldn't hope to compete, the best tactic was to be different—totally different.

She twisted and turned in front of the mirror, trying to get a glimpse of herself from every angle. What would Rhys think of it? Would he like it? It was disturbing to have to admit how important it was to her that he should.

The past few days had been far from easy. Oh, they had managed to live in a reasonably civilised fashion—working and eating and sleeping in the tiny cottage without any major conflict arising—but the tension between them had been sizzling beneath the surface, waiting for the slightest spark to make it explode.

She really wasn't looking forward to this evening—but it was no good trying to hide in here. A swift glance at her watch—the only jewellery she was wearing, apart from her favourite tiny gold swallow earrings—told her that it was time to go. Squaring her shoulders, she faced her reflection in the mirror.

'You can do it, girl,' she admonished herself sternly. 'You've faced wars and famines, angry politicians and armed drug-dealers—tonight should be a piece of cake.'

But she had an uncomfortable feeling that Helena Gillam-Fox might prove to be a more formidable opponent than any of the characters she had encountered in the more dramatic moments of her career. With a sigh she picked up the slim black patent leather clutch-bag that Carole had sent to go with the suit, and, turning from the mirror, stepped out to face the fray.

Rhys was reading the paper as she walked down the stairs. He glanced up, one level eyebrow lifting in frank surprise as he saw her. He put the paper aside, those cool grey eyes surveying her slowly from head to toe and back again. 'Well... Not quite what I was expecting, but certainly...different,' he accorded, with a smile that added layers of meaning to his words.

'Are you...ready to go?' she asked, her voice a little unsteady.

'Certainly.' He rose lazily to his feet. He too was wearing a formal dinner jacket, elegantly tailored to mould across the impressive breadth of his shoulders, with a pristine white silk shirt and crisp black bow-tie completing the formal effect. With a sudden dry-mouthed intensity Lynne felt the intriguing contrast between his big, hard-muscled male frame and her own slight, dainty stature—a contrast heightened by the similarity of the clothes they were wearing.

With an impeccable politeness that she sensed held a hint of mockery he opened the front door for her, waiting while she locked it, and then held open the passenger door of his car. This wasn't the bland, expensive, modern chunk of metal she had envisaged him of owning, but a classic Jaguar two-seater sports car, built the year before the Second World War but still in near perfect condition.

She had seen it parked outside the cottage, and had admired it, with its long, elegant bonnet and gleaming dark green paintwork, binnacle-style headlamps and wide running-boards down each side. 'It's like stepping through a time-warp,' she approved now, unable to resist touching the helm-sized steering wheel. 'Back to when cars were really cars.'

He slanted her a faintly sardonic smile. 'I'm glad you like it.'

She shrugged, unaccountably reluctant to share any point of agreement with him—it felt a good deal safer when they were arguing. 'I'd still rather have my little bean-can,' she insisted. 'At least I'm not worried all the time that someone might pinch it.'

'Oh, I doubt anyone would steal this,' he responded drily. 'And if they did they wouldn't get very far in it—it isn't the sort of car you'd go joyriding in.'

Lynne soon discovered what he meant. The two point five litre engine still produced a fair turn of speed, but it was clear that the car was something of a handful to drive—she certainly wouldn't have wanted to tackle it, particularly on the switchback roads of rural Cornwall. The advantage was that he was having to concentrate to the exclusion of making conversation, so she was able to sit back in her seat and relax a little.

She was trying not to think about the evening ahead—it would only make her even more nervous. She should never have let him inveigle her into coming. The last thing she needed was to find herself caught in the crossfire between Rhys and his wife—ex-wife...whatever... She had an uncomfortable feeling that she was going to be the one who came off worst.

Oak House stood on the fringes of a small village a few miles west of Bath. Solidly built of rust-coloured brick at the height of the Victorian era, it was the kind of house described by up-market estate agents as 'a desirable gentleman's residence'. Ordered symmetry was the predominant feature, from the neatly clipped yew hedge to the leaded carriage-lamps on each side of the front door.

'I had no idea the Brigadier had so many close friends,' Rhys remarked drily as he parked the car on the gravel carriage-sweep next to a row of BMWs and Volvos.

Lynne said nothing, hurrying to climb out of the car before he came round to assist her. Their feet crunched slightly on the well-tended gravel as they walked up to the front door. Rhys rang the doorbell, and as its chimes echoed somewhere in the house she drew in a long, deep, steadying breath, struggling for some semblance of composure with which to arm herself for the coming ordeal.

Beside her, Rhys laughed softly; the glint of mocking amusement in those hard grey eyes told her that he knew exactly why she was so on edge. 'You know, that little bow's really rather fetching,' he murmured, tipping the satin bow-tie with one finger. He smiled slowly, holding her captive with that mesmerising gaze. 'There's something incredibly sexy about a woman wearing a man's clothes.' His voice was low and husky, and as she stood there helpless in the grip of the spell he was weaving around her, he let his finger trail down over her heated skin, tracing the line of her lapel right down into the soft cleft of shadow between her breasts. *Incredibly* sexy...'

His head bent over hers and she felt the brush of his mouth over her trembling lips, his sensuous tongue tracing their contours, coaxing them apart. It was a kiss of the sweetest tenderness but Lynne felt as if her heart was going to break—because she knew exactly why he was doing it.

She knew, but couldn't stop him, so needy in her hunger for his kiss that she was letting him use her in his cruel games with his ex-wife. She heard footsteps approaching inside the house, heard the door open; and as he drew her closer against him, ruthlessly plundering the sweet valley of her mouth and stirring the inevitable response, she heard someone laugh, startled and a little shocked.

'Really, darling, do be a little more discreet,' Helena protested, her cool amusement calling his bluff. 'You'll smudge the poor girl's lipstick.'

He took his time in letting Lynne go, his hard mouth curving into a smile of mocking satisfaction. 'Good evening, Helena. You're looking incredibly beautiful tonight, as usual.'

She was—in the sort of slim black off-the-shoulder number that Lynne would have loved to be able to wear, if only she were a little taller. Her rich ash-blonde hair was swept up into an elegant pile of curls on top of her head, and the three-strand pearl choker encircling her slender throat was undoubtedly genuine. And that perfectly applied lipstick would never dare smudge.

'Thank you,' she responded, all smiling charm. 'Well, don't stand there on the doorstep—it's dreadfully cold. Your father is in the drawing-room. He's waiting for you—you *are* a little late.' She swept regally across the imposing hall, leaving them to follow in her wake.

Lynne felt the pressure of Rhys's hand in the small of her back as for a moment she resisted. But it was too late now for last-minute reservations. Feeling like an aristocrat taking that last walk to the guillotine, she moved reluctantly forward. Helena had thrown open a pair of wide oak doors, and Lynne had a brief impression of a rather grand room, with a high ceiling and tall windows, its walls hung with a collection of sombre oil-paintings in heavy gilt frames.

But she had little time to study the décor; the conversation in the room had ceased abruptly as they'd entered, and it seemed as if a hundred pairs of eyes had turned to stare at them as they stood hesitantly on the threshold—though in reality there were barely more than a dozen people in the room.

It crossed her mind that it was rather a formal gathering for a family party—she suspected that was Helena's influence. The men all wore dinner jackets while the ladies vied with each other in the elegance of their gowns. If it hadn't been for Carole's distinctive choice of outfit, she would have faded into insignificance in such splendid company, Lynne acknowledged wryly.

But there was little danger of that—and not just because of her unconventional attire, she realised as Rhys drew her forward. The awkward silence continued as everyone stared, then came a few whispered comments as those who didn't know the situation were quickly put in the picture. And, just in case anyone was still in any doubt, Rhys let his hand slip down her spine to rest far too intimately over the smooth curve of her *derrière*, let his eyes linger over her shoulder and down into the secret, shadowy valley between her breasts.

She felt a hot blush steal up over her cheeks, acutely conscious of the picture they must present, framed in the doorway—the eldest son of the house with his recently discarded wife on one arm and his new mistress on the other. Which had been exactly his intention, she reminded herself bitterly; how could she possibly be in love with someone who was capable of that kind of ruthlessness?

If Helena was embarrassed, however, she was well able to conceal it—that cool poise didn't even waver. 'Lynne, my dear, I'm sure you'll want to...er...comb your hair before we sit down to dinner,' she said graciously. 'Let me show you the way.'

Lynne gritted her teeth into a passable semblance of a smile; perhaps she ought to be grateful that Rhys's ex-wife was being so gracious, but instead she found it overbearing—she really needed no demonstration of how much more worthy the other woman was of being at his side. And she wasn't fooled by that pose of smiling tolerance—it really was a little too saccharine to be believed. Helena Gillam-Fox was a lady who was accustomed to getting what she wanted—and what she wanted at the moment was her husband back.

'What a clever little suit,' Helena purred in generous approval as she led the way up the wide sweep of the stairs and along a carpeted corridor. 'I would never have thought of wearing something like that.'

'Thank you,' Lynne responded warily, sensing a two-edged compliment.

'You know, my dear, I'm really not surprised that my husband should be infatuated with you,' she went on, in a honeyed tone that made Lynne's hackles start to rise. 'You're very sweet, and very pretty, and you've come into his life at a moment when he doesn't quite know what he's looking for. But I would hate you to be hurt when he begins to realise what really matters.'

'I appreciate your concern,' Lynne countered stiffly. 'But I assure you I can take care of myself.'

'That's good.' Such a polite conversation. Such treacherous shoals beneath the surface. She opened a door, showing Lynne into a large bedroom with walls of gleaming panelled wood and a high coved ceiling, furnished with exquisite taste. 'This is my favourite room,' Helena said sweetly. 'Rhys and I always use it when we visit the Brigadier. Do make yourself comfortable—the bathroom is through that door. I'll see you downstairs in a few moments.'

She swept out, leaving a lingering hint of expensive perfume behind her. Lynne glanced wryly around the room. She was under no misapprehensions—she had been brought in here quite intentionally. She had been meant to notice the delicate French silk nightgown drifting negligently across the rose damask silk of the bedspread, the silver-framed photograph on the bedside table.

Her soft mouth twisted into a crooked smile as she picked up the photograph and studied it. The happy couple—she seated, he standing behind her, one hand resting possessively on her shoulder. Two beautiful people, a little aloof from the rest of the world, meant to be together. And anyone who wished it weren't so was heading for heartbreak.

CHAPTER EIGHT

THE dining-room of Oak House was as imposing as the drawing-room—Lynne had the feeling of being in a museum rather than a private house. The dining-table was quite large enough to seat the sixteen people around it in comfort, and the light of two heavy crystal chandeliers sparkled on a treasure-trove of silverware and fine Royal Doulton porcelain.

At least she had been seated next to Rhys—she suspected that Helena would have preferred to separate them, but the dictates of social etiquette had triumphed over her personal wishes.

The Brigadier, of course, was at the head of the table. An older version of his elder son, age had sculpted the hard bones of his face into forbidding crags. And he had an equally irascible temper, to judge by his reaction when his critical scrutiny of the table setting had detected that some of the forks were millimetrically misaligned. But he also had an unexpected sense of humour, barking with laughter whenever he was amused.

He was laughing now at something Rhys had said. 'Ah, yes—that was the finest damned battle I ever fought!' he declared richly. 'We were just talking about the time they tried to demolish the old barracks and stick us in some damned modern thing,' he explained to the company at large. 'Dare say Rhys has told you all about it, m'dear,' he added to Lynne.

Helena's soft laugh interrupted him. 'Oh, but, Brigadier, you're forgetting—Lynne and Rhys haven't known each other very long. I'm sure they haven't had the time to talk about things like that.'

Lynne felt her cheeks blush a hot pink at the unmistakable innuendo, but Rhys was quite untroubled. 'On the contrary,' he put in smoothly. 'We met—when was it, Lynne?—about eighteen months ago now.'

She flashed him a fulminating glare. 'Very briefly,' she conceded.

His smile was wicked. 'One long, unforgettable night,' he murmured, with an air of pleasurable reminiscence.

Lynne had some difficulty in suppressing a fierce desire to kick him beneath the table. 'I'm a journalist,' she explained crisply. 'I was about to interview Vice-President Santos the day he had to skip the country so urgently, and I ended up going with them.'

'That's right,' Rhys conceded wryly. 'It was Lynne who got me down to hospital in San Leopoldo with a bullet in my leg. If it hadn't been for her, I could have bled to death.'

'It wasn't particularly difficult,' she countered, slanting him a brittle smile. 'You'd told me we were a hundred miles from anywhere, but it turned out that the city was only round the next bend in the river— barely five miles away.'

He laughed with lazy mockery, unfazed by the accusation. 'I was speaking figuratively.'

'Ah...' Helena's cool poise was showing signs of slipping, but with a visible effort of will she pulled it back together. 'So you're a journalist? How interesting. That must be a very demanding career.'

'It can be at times,' Lynne acknowledged steadily.

'It must make it...difficult to sustain a relationship, though, with the hours being so unpredictable. I imagine the divorce rate must be pretty high? Doesn't that worry you?'

'Not really.' The opportunity to dig back at Rhys for using her so ruthlessly to score points off his wife was irresistible. 'I'm not particularly interested in getting married, and any man I have a...relationship with has to understand that my career comes first.'

Helena looked a little startled, but then she smiled,

barely able to conceal a certain smugness. 'Of course. Though it really wouldn't do if we all felt like that, would it? What ever would all the poor men do if we weren't there to take care of them?'

Lynne lifted one sardonic eyebrow. 'I really don't know,' she countered. 'Take care of themselves, perhaps?'

She was surprised to hear the sound of clapping from further along the table, and glanced around to see that it was Rhys's sister-in-law, Fiona, who had responded. 'Well said!' she approved, leaning forward, her eyes dancing merrily. 'Though most of them would probably starve to death inside a month.'

Lynne was grateful that the conversation lapsed after that, turning to other subjects and allowing her to draw out of it. It had perhaps been a little foolish of her to clash with Helena in that way, but she had had just about enough of her. The other woman had swiftly recovered from the dent in her composure, and was bathing everyone around her in the radiance of her charm. Was it only her jealousy that made her dislike the woman so intensely? Did everyone else think she was wonderful?

She slanted a swift glance up at Rhys and caught the glint of dry humour in his eyes as he looked back at her. At least the evening was turning out to someone's satisfaction, she reflected with a touch of asperity. He had given in to his ex-wife's insistence that he should come tonight, but he had made very sure that it wouldn't turn out the way she had planned.

But would he go back to her eventually, once he had tired of playing his bachelor games? Maybe... And in the meantime Helena was being very clever, loosening the leash, avoiding making a scene. It was the kind of strategy she herself had tried to use with Paul—being patient, waiting. It hadn't worked for her, but it wouldn't surprise her if Helena had better luck.

The food was excellent. They had started with scallops sautéed in butter, served with a salad of endive and chives, followed by a tender fillet of lamb in Madeira sauce and finishing with a syllabub flavoured delicately with ginger. Lynne strongly detected the influence of Helena over the menu—the Brigadier, she suspected, would have chosen good, plain English cooking.

It was Helena who finally took it upon herself to draw the meal to an end, rising gracefully to her feet. 'Well, ladies,' she announced, with a smile that anticipated no possibility of argument, 'shall we do the traditional thing, and leave the gentlemen to their cigars?'

With murmurs of assent and a shifting of chairs, the women all took advantage of the suggestion to withdraw discreetly and tidy themselves up. Lynne felt obliged to follow, but as she was walking up the stairs she felt a hand on her arm and turned in surprise to see Fiona, the wife of Rhys's younger brother Simon, smiling at her merrily.

'Come with me,' she said in a conspiratorial whisper. 'You don't want to give that bitch another chance to have a dig at you.'

Bemused, Lynne followed her to another room, further along the passage—not quite so large or as beautifully furnished as Helena's, and bearing the signs of being inhabited by a man who was accustomed to having a batman to tidy up after him and a woman who had no intention of taking over the task. Fiona flopped down on the bed and kicked off her shoes.

'That's better! I hate wearing heels—barbaric fashion! And we thought the Chinese were cruel for binding women's feet! I'm sorry about all this,' she went on as Lynne struggled to keep up with her quicksilver flow of conversation. 'I shouldn't really have given her the chance to take over like this, but I'm afraid I'm not very good at standing up to La Belle Helena when she's got the bit between her teeth—I'd rather be run over by a truck. Not that I ever have been run over by a truck,' she added blithely. 'But I'm inclined to think it would be far less painful.'

Lynne laughed, glad to be able to relax a little at last. In any other company, this laughing young woman would have been notably attractive, with her flame-red hair and light dusting of freckles, though beside Helena Gillam-Fox she appeared almost gauche and provincial.

'Si tells me you own the cottage where Rhys is staying,' Fiona bounced on. 'It sounds smashing—right on the edge of the cliff like that. It must have a fabulous view in the summer.'

'Yes, it does,' Lynne confirmed, smiling. 'You must come down and visit some time.'

'Oh, yes! I'd love that!' Fiona sat up again, and reached across to the dressing-table for a hairbrush, dragging it through her amazing curls in a vain effort to bring them under control. 'Oh, hell—it's never going to look presentable,' she sighed. 'Not like Helena's hair—that's always perfect.'

Lynne smiled drily. 'I gather she's not your favourite person?'

'I hate her guts!' Fiona admitted with a chuckle. 'You wouldn't believe how chuffed I was that Rhys brought you along tonight! I suppose I ought to feel sorry for her, really—she's gone to all this trouble, only to have you put her nose out of joint.'

'I'm not really sure that I've done that,' Lynne demurred, shaking her head.

'Oh, she'll live to fight another day,' Fiona admitted cheerfully. 'But at least she might finally begin to realise that Rhys really is serious this time—he's not going to go back to her.'

'Isn't he?' Lynne queried, her voice tinged with wistful doubt.

Fiona shook her head firmly. 'Not this time. He's put up with more than enough from her over the years, but when she asked him for a divorce... Well, she went too far.'

'She asked *him* for a divorce?'

'That's right.' Fiona slanted her a searching look. 'Didn't you know about it?' She cast a swift glance towards the door. 'I suppose I shouldn't really be telling you this,' she went on, lowering her voice, 'but she was having an affair at the time. *Not* her first affair, I might add—she's had quite a few. Mostly I suspect she was trying to make Rhys jealous, bring him to heel, but she never had much success with that tactic. Anyway, she actually told Rhys she wanted a divorce while he was still in hospital, when they thought he was going to lose his leg.' Her mouth set into a hard line. 'She said she didn't want to be married to a...cripple.'

'She *what*?' Lynne breathed, her eyes widening in shock. 'The...bitch!'

Fiona nodded. 'The only people Rhys told about it were me and Si. Anyway, first her lover decided he wasn't going to leave his wife after all, and then Rhys started to have all this success with his books, so she changed her mind. The trouble is, she always has managed to get her own way, and she simply refused to believe it—even when he got the divorce.'

'Well, I suppose if he was in love with her...'

Fiona tipped her head on one side, thinking about that one. 'To be honest, I'm not sure that he ever was,' she mused. 'It was more the old man's idea—the Brigadier's. He and her father are bosom buddies from when they were at Sandhurst together, and they dreamed up this stupid romantic notion one night on the Western Front, or something. Apparently they decided that if one of them had a son and the other one a daughter, the two unfortunate offspring were supposed to get married—to seal the bond of friendship, as it were. Anyway, Helena was all for it—she had her eye on Rhys from when she was about five! He was a very good catch, of course—so good-looking! Even when we were teenagers, all the girls used to fancy him like mad. But even so, it took her an awfully long time to get him to the altar—they were running bets on whether or not she'd ever succeed!'

'You mean...he married her just to please his father?' Lynne protested, a note of scepticism in her voice.

'More or less. Simon told me the Brigadier had arranged for Rhys to be offered a commission in his old regiment—without telling him about it. When Rhys turned it down, the old man hit the roof. So I think marrying Helena was a kind of gesture of appeasement. Maybe he thought he'd get a bit of peace, after her chasing him for all those years, but instead she started nagging him to leave the Army—said she didn't want to be the wife of a sergeant...'

'Ah, there you are.' The door had swung silently open behind them. 'You've been gone so long, I thought you'd got lost.' Rhys was smiling, but the glint in those hard grey eyes warned Lynne that he had heard enough to know what they had been talking about—and the hint of menace in that velvet-smooth voice did not bode well.

'Oh...we were just...chatting,' she responded, feeling the hot blush of guilt creep up over her cheeks.

'Really? And when you girls get chatting you just don't know when to stop, do you?'

Fiona laughed, undisturbed by his grim sarcasm. 'Heavens, is that the time? I didn't realise we'd been up here so long! I'd better get downstairs, or the Brigadier will have polished off all the brandy and be telling one of his dreadful stories!'

She skipped away, leaving Lynne alone to face the music.

'Well... So I was right all along,' he grated in a voice of jagged steel. 'Never trust a journalist. I suppose I shouldn't really be surprised that you should snatch at the first chance you get to pump one of my family. Did you find out everything you wanted to know? Knowing Fiona, she's probably given you enough to fill a whole Sunday supplement!'

Lynne didn't reply. She really couldn't blame him for being so angry, she acknowledged wryly; it must seem to him that all his suspicions were being confirmed. He certainly wasn't going to believe her excuses—even if she could bring herself to tell him that her interest in him was purely personal.

'Come on,' he rapped out, turning sharply on his heel. 'I'm getting you out of here before you do any more damage.'

With some reluctance, Lynne followed him. She would have liked a chance at least to say goodbye to the Brigadier and Fiona, but she was unpleasantly aware that Rhys's reaction to the idea was not likely to be very favourable. But as they reached the bottom of the stairs Helena came out into the hall.

'Oh, dear, you're leaving already?' she protested, her honeyed voice conveying just the right degree of dignified disappointment, though the gleam of malice in her eyes betrayed her truer nature.

'I'm afraid so,' Rhys responded tonelessly. 'We...have a long drive ahead of us.'

'If you'd agreed to stay the night, you wouldn't have to dash away,' she purred on a note of gentle reproof.

His grim smile said everything. 'I don't think so. Goodnight, Helena.'

'Goodnight, darling. See you soon.'

He slanted her a sardonic look and didn't even bother to answer, simply placing a dry kiss on her cheek.

'Goodnight...er...Lynne.' The smile was patronising, almost pitying. 'It was *so* nice meeting you.'

'And you,' Lynne returned with bite. 'Goodnight.'

Somehow she managed to put one foot in front of the other as they walked out to the car. It had started to rain, cold needles whipped up by the wind and stinging her face as she waited for Rhys to open the passenger door for her. A dark, stormy night—but not as dark and stormy as the look in those narrowed eyes.

She had tossed her quilted jacket into the back earlier, expecting that she would probably need it, and she was glad now that she had as she huddled into it and slid into the leather seat, watching as he walked round the bonnet to climb in beside her. Though the shivers running through her were not entirely due to the damp chill in the air.

He turned the ignition and slid the car into gear, reversing back out of the space and turning the car towards the wrought-iron gates that led out onto the road. It would take them about three hours to get back to Porthwyk, and with Rhys in his present frame of mind it was not going to be a pleasant drive.

From beneath her lashes, she slanted a cautious look up at him, studying that hard profile, the grim line of his mouth. There had been little enough chance, she knew, that anything deeper could grow out of that sizzling spark of sexual attraction between them, but even that remote possibility had now been destroyed.

Her conversation with Fiona was still echoing in her mind. It had certainly given her plenty to think about, completely overturning the picture she had had of Rhys's marriage and the reason for his divorce. She had thought it must have been because he was incapable of making a commitment, but it seemed that he had tried hard to make the marriage work—it had only been Helena's unforgivable behaviour that had forced him to end it.

She felt her jaw tighten on a sudden wave of anger. No wonder he had wanted to appear tonight with a new 'mistress' on his arm—the blow to his male pride, especially at a time when he had been at his most vulnerable, afraid that he might become permanently disabled, must have been cruel beyond words. Tonight had been an unmissable opportunity for him to demonstrate to Helena that he no longer cared.

But he did, she mused wistfully; he might try to deny it, even to himself, but he was still caught up in her web, unable to break free. Didn't she know only too well that love left scars that took a long time to heal? It had taken her months to get over Paul—even though, as she now knew, she had never really been in love with him.

Oh, she had been flattered that he should pick her out, when he could have had almost any woman he chose. And he had manipulated her very skilfully with promises and uncertainty, creating a destructive habit of insecurity and illusion to keep her around for as long as it had suited him.

But it hadn't been love. She knew what the real thing was now.

It was after midnight by the time they reached the coast road above Porthwyk. Lynne could hear the roar of the sea above the sound of the car's engine, and in the intermittent moonlight she could see that it was rough out there—maybe not quite as rough as the night she had arrived, but certainly not a night to go for a midnight swim.

She was about to wonder aloud if the lifeboat was out when from the harbour master's office down in the village a point of light streaked up into the sky, swiftly followed by another, and the twin boom of the maroons echoed along the cliffs.

Her heart thudded sharply against her ribs. There was no need to ask the question that sprang to her lips; Rhys's face was set with that look she had seen before as he put his foot on the accelerator, speeding the car down the hill. As it bounced over the cobbles along the harbour-front they passed Dennis, fighting his way into a thick sweater as he ran from the flat over his father's garage.

Rhys slowed beside him. 'Jump on!'

'Thanks, mate,' the young mechanic responded breathlessly, skipping onto the running-board and holding on grimly to anything he could grab as they swung up the hill towards the boathouse.

By the time they reached it quite a few of the crew were already there, and others were arriving—running, cycling, coming by car—whatever it took to get there.

Curran was already in his yellow oilskins, yelling at the others to hurry as they raced into the crew-room, stripping off jackets and sweaters as they ran, somehow managing not to bump into each other in spite of the limited space.

'OK...Dennis, Harry, Rhys... Thought you was off watch tonight?' Curran queried as he checked the muster.

'Just got back,' Rhys responded, sliding his feet into a pair of yellow seaboots. He straightened, his eyes meeting Lynne's in a single exchange that might have meant everything or nothing. 'Take the car home,' was all he said, tossing her the keys. And then he was gone, up the ladder onto the deck, and disappearing into the bright orange cabin.

'Right boys—ready to go?' called Curran. 'Clear the links.'

Creaking, the heavy winch drew the big boat back on the slipway, easing the strong chains that held her. One of the shore team humped the thick links aside, and at Curran's next command Dennis fired the engines into life. Lynne stood in the doorway of the crew-room, her mouth dry as she gazed up at the sleek blue hull; inside the boathouse it looked huge, but out there on that unforgiving grey ocean beyond the wide double doors it would be no more than a bobbing coracle.

'Let her go!'

Another of the shore team knocked out the retaining pin with a sledgehammer. At first, as everyone waited tensely, nothing seemed to be happening, and then slowly the boat began to glide, majestic at first, then gaining speed under its own momentum as it slid down the long wooden slipway. Lynne caught a last brief glimpse of Rhys, adjusting something on the VHF direction-finder above his head, before the bows hit the water.

For one heart-stopping moment the boat appeared to sink. But then she surfaced in a magnificent surge, water streaming from her decks as she rode triumphantly over the waves, curving out and away on a line that would take her clear of the headland. A cheer went up from those remaining behind; however many times she watched that spectacle, Lynne knew she would never fail to feel the raw impact on her emotions.

After all the noise and drama of the launch, the quietness that followed had an air of anti-climax. More of the crew than were needed had turned out for the shout, and those that were left behind, disappointed at missing the action, moved around helping the shore team tidy up the boathouse, checking the winch and chain, while a couple of the wives who had come down to watch the boat go out started to pick up the hurriedly discarded clothes from the floor in the crew-room and put them away in the long cupboard where the oilskins were stored.

'Six minutes and twenty-two seconds exactly,' announced Barney Pinch, the elderly harbour master, consulting his stopwatch. 'Not bad—could be better.'

'What is it?' Lynne enquired diffidently, not sure whether it was the proper etiquette to ask.

'Coastguard got a report of a rowboat drifting out beyond Castle Head. We were put on twenty minutes' stand-by, but Curran decided to take her straight out. Could be something, could be nothing.'

Lynne gazed out of the window at the wide expanse of darkness beyond the sheltered cove. 'A rowing-boat? How on earth will they find something as small as that?' she mused, half to herself. 'There's miles of ocean out there.'

'Aye, it's a bit like looking for a needle in a haystack—only wetter,' Barney chuckled. 'I've known 'em be out for twenty-four hours and then come up with nothing more than an old tractor tyre. Still, you never know—can't take no risks.' The short-wave radio on the desk beside him crackled, and Lynne heard voices. Barney chuckled again. 'That'll upset 'em,' he declared. 'They've scrambled a Sea King helicopter from Culdrose. It's a bit of a contest between them and the boat whenever there's a shout—friendly, like, but it keeps 'em on their toes.'

Lynne was studying the powerful radio. 'You can talk to the boat from here?' she asked.

'Can do. Don't generally, though—not while the action's going on. I just listen in. They'll be in direct contact with MR Sub—Maritime Rescue Sub-Centre, that is. They co-ordinate everything, and they're in charge till the boat gets close enough to make contact with the distressed vessel itself. I may get a call when they're on their way home—especially if they need the ambulance or something. I keep a log here, and make a note of who's gone out so they get their expenses. That's it, really.' His faded eyes took on a faraway look as he gazed out of the window towards the distant, dark horizon. 'Wish I was out there with 'em, though,' he sighed softly. 'Miss it, I do. It's been nearly twenty years now...'

Lynne followed the direction of his gaze. They all seemed to have it, these men of the lifeboat—almost an addiction to the dangerous job they undertook: a job that had to take precedence over anything else, that could demand their instant attendance at any time of the day or night, seven days a week, fifty-two weeks of the year, for a payment that was no more than a token gesture. That was what brought them all racing down here whenever their pager buzzed or they heard the sound of the maroons over the harbour, never knowing what awaited them out there on the stormy ocean—never knowing for sure that they would come back.

That thought made her shiver; if anything went wrong out there tonight, if for any reason Rhys didn't come home, she would have to live for ever with the knowledge that they had parted in anger, with so many stupid misunderstandings still lying between them. And she had never told him that she loved him...

Not that she would have been able to tell him anyway, she reflected, her heart twisting in pain—it wasn't what he wanted, and to be fair he had never asked for it. He wanted only a light-hearted affair, something simple and uncomplicated, to help him heal the wounds the breakup of his marriage had inflicted. He wouldn't want the responsibility of having her love him.

Dammit, what was wrong with her that she couldn't prevent her foolish heart making choices that her head told her were all wrong? But reason had nothing to do with love. It could strike like a virus, producing its own sweet fever—and, heaven help her, she never wanted to recover from it.

From the radio came another metallic crackle, and then she heard Rhys's voice, distorted by the atmospherics but clearly discernible. 'Porthwyk lifeboat to coastguard. Porthwyk lifeboat to coastguard. Can you update the lat and long for us, please? Over.'

'Roger, Porthwyk lifeboat,' came the calm response. 'That's fifty degrees forty-two north, by four degrees fifty-five west. Over.'

'Roger, coastguard. ETA thirty minutes—repeat, thirty minutes. Over and out.'

Lynne gazed at the radio as it fell silent—it seemed like her one concrete link with him, even though she couldn't talk to him and he had no idea that she was still here listening. A fierce gust of wind rattled the corrugated iron roof of the boathouse; what must it be like out there, in the inky darkness and driving rain, riding those steep, rolling waves? Her eyes lifted again to the horizon, scanning it as if by her will alone she could somehow keep him safe.

'Well, looks like we could be in for an all-nighter,' Barney declared, bending to light a Calor-gas heater next to the desk and pulling a battered copy of the local paper from his pocket. 'No telling.'

'Yes. Well, I...suppose I'd better go home.' Lynne turned reluctantly away from the window. 'Goodnight, Barney.'

''Night, lovey. And don't you go worrying yourself

about your chap,' he added, a kindly twinkle in his eyes. 'They'll be all right out there. There's no one knows these waters like old Curran.'

She smiled, trying to tell herself that she should be reassured by that. But as she climbed into Rhys's car she couldn't avert her eyes from that dark, unforgiving sweep of ocean out beyond the shelter of the headland. The thought of something happening to him was like a physical pain, cutting into her heart.

The wind was still rattling the rain against the windows of the cottage. Lynne hadn't bothered to go to bed; she wouldn't sleep—couldn't sleep—until she knew Rhys was safely back on dry land. Pacing around the kitchen with a mug of cocoa in her hands, she sighed impatiently. She might as well be back down at the boathouse—at least there she would know immediately what was going on.

Wrapped up warmly, in a woollen shirt and thick cardigan under her quilted jacket, she drove the short distance down the hill in her own car. It was past three in the morning, and most of the village was asleep. Quietly she pushed open the door of the crew-room. Barney was dozing over his newspaper, but he came to and glanced up, grinning when he saw her.

'Couldn't sleep?' he queried with gentle understanding.

Lynne shook her head wryly. 'No. I... Would it be all right for me to stay?' she asked diffidently.

''Course it would, lovey. I could do with the company. Put the kettle on, there's a good lass—let's have a nice cup of tea.'

She did as he asked, glad to have someone to talk to, something to do. 'Any news yet?' she enquired.

'Not yet. They're around the spot where the flare was spotted, but, what with the wind-drift and currents, the boat or whatever it was could be miles away by now.'

Lynne nodded, making herself concentrate on

making the tea as she tried not to let herself worry. The kettle was on an old kitchen table in the corner, along with a stained teatray and a dozen or so thick mugs. 'Where's the teapot?' she asked over her shoulder as she filled the kettle and plugged it in.

'Oh, we don't bother with nothing fancy like that, lovey,' Barney responded, tickled. 'Just drop the teabag straight in the mug. I like mine good and strong, with plenty of sugar.'

She made it the way he liked it, and her own a little weaker. The milk was from a carton of long-life, and she didn't care to enquire how long it had been there. She carried the mugs over to the desk and put them down.

'Ah, good girl,' Barney approved, sniffing at the rich brew and taking a speculative sip as if it were the finest vintage wine. 'You make a good cup of tea, I'll say that for you. Fetch up a chair, then—might as well keep yourself warm.'

It was peaceful, sitting there in the circle of light cast by the lamp on Barney's desk, huddled close to the puttering Calor-gas heater, listening to the sound of the rain drumming softly on the tin roof, the wind rattling the shutters of the window and the constant rolling roar of the sea below them. From time to time the radio would crackle into life, with some exchange of information between the searchers out at sea and the district controller at the Maritime Rescue Sub-Centre, and her heart would crease every time she heard Rhys's voice.

And Barney told her stories—wonderful ancient stories—full of giants and fairy-folk, mermaids and piskies, interspersed with legends of the smugglers and wreckers who had once haunted these rugged coasts. As she listened she remembered the stories of her childhood, how she had loved nothing better than to tuck under the bedclothes with a book and a torch, reading long after she was supposed to have gone to sleep.

Maybe... Could she try writing something like that? She had never thought of writing for children, but she seemed to be wasting her time with the book she had been planning to write; she was still barely a third of the way through the first chapter, and yesterday afternoon she had dozed off to sleep over it—if *she* was that bored by it, what could she expect of a prospective reader? Perhaps she ought to try something completely different...

It must have been more than an hour before there was a crackle of voices from the radio which made Barney prick up his ears. 'They've found 'em—sounds like it was the boys in the chopper.' He bent over the radio, listening intently. 'Aye—two lads, it is, by the sound of it. They're just winching 'em aboard. Our boys'll be on their way home now.'

Almost as he spoke, Rhys's voice, with its strange, metallic distortion, came over the airwaves. 'Porthwyk lifeboat to shore-base. Wake up, Barney, you old salt, and get the kettle on. We're coming in.'

Thirty minutes later the boathouse was once again alive with noise as the crew stumped around, stripping off their wet oilskins and hanging them to dry, laughing and joking with the release of tension. The lifeboat was tied up at the bottom of the ramp, waiting for morning, when she would be hosed down and then winched back up into the shed.

Lynne had been the one to put the kettle on, having seven mugs of thick tea ready as the men had trudged up the ramp—one for each of the crew and one for Barney. Rhys had taken his mug from her with no more than a word of thanks, just like the others—if he had been surprised that she was there, he hadn't shown it.

He was busy with Curran and Barney now, finishing off the log; he hadn't said anything about her waiting for him, but he hadn't told her not to, either, so she was just trying to make herself useful in her own small way—taking the mugs back from the crew as they finished their tea, washing them up, drying them on a teatowel and then lining them up again on the rickety table where she had found them.

'Thanks, lassy.' Dennis grinned as he handed her his empty mug. 'You're doing a grand job there.'

'Oh, I just thought I'd help out if I could,' she responded lightly, aware of the steely glint of Rhys's eyes stabbing suddenly across the room.

'How's the car going?' Dennis enquired.

'Much better since you had a look at it, thank you,' she returned, refusing to allow Rhys to dictate to her, even silently, whom she could or could not be friends with. 'I must have had half a dozen different garages try to fix it up in London, but not one of them seemed to have a clue.'

'Ah, well, I've been around engines all my life, see.' Dennis beamed, delighted at the praise. 'They're like babies to me—each one of 'em different, each with their own little ways. You have to coax 'em to get the best out of 'em. These fancy London chaps, they might have all the training and that, but it's just an engine to them, a bit of old metal. Me, I love 'em.'

'Well, it certainly works!' Lynne laughed—and in spite of her efforts to ignore the knot of tension in her stomach it was a nervous, edgy sound. 'I haven't had a bit of trouble with it.'

Rhys had finished what he was doing and risen to his feet. 'Are you off home, then, Dennis?' he enquired pointedly.

The young Cornishman couldn't fail to pick up the signals. He glanced from one to the other and then grinned a little sheepishly. 'I reckon so,' he conceded. 'I'll be down in the morning to help winch up the boat, Curran.'

'OK, mate. Goodnight, then.'

'I'll finish up here and lock up,' Rhys suggested to Curran and Barney. 'You two get along home.'

The elderly harbour master ran a hand across his

tired eyes. 'Are you sure?' he demurred, though there was a note of gratitude in his voice.

'Of course. Go on, the pair of you—you could both do with some sleep.'

'Right, then. Well, see you in the morning, boy. 'Night, Lynne—and thanks for all the tea.'

Lynne could only smile a little unsteadily, waving her hand in farewell as the two older men departed, leaving her alone with Rhys. He glanced briefly across at her, his hard mouth still set in that grim line. 'I'll just check that the boatdoors are secure, and then we can be going,' he said.

She nodded dumbly, and bent her head to concentrate on fastening the buttons of her jacket. He was still angry, and she probably couldn't blame him. Impatiently she scrubbed away the tears she didn't want him to see. It probably wasn't the time for a confrontation now, but tomorrow—or rather today—he would probably tell her that he was leaving; moving out of the cottage, out of her life. It would be better that way, she tried to tell herself, though with little conviction. The longer this situation went on, the harder it would be when it was over.

CHAPTER NINE

THE storm had ebbed a little, but the wind was still blowing a gale as they stepped outside. Lynne pulled the hood of her jacket up over her head, waiting at the bottom of the steps as Rhys locked the door of the boathouse—he had kept his yellow oilskin coat on over his dinner jacket, the collar turned up against the wind.

The waves were still pounding against the rocks below them, churning around the bottom of the lifeboat ramp, where the boat was tied up and dancing on her ropes as she rode out the worst of the weather. Lynne walked over to the rail, fascinated by the sheer power of the untamed elements. The salt spray was stinging cold against her face, but she didn't care—it made her feel as if she were almost part of it, the wild turmoil of the sea matching the turmoil of emotion in her heart.

The sound of a footfall close behind her made her turn her head. Against the light of the single streetlamp that burned on the corner, Rhys looked taller, broader than ever. Quickly she turned away again, gripping the rail. 'Will she...be all right there—the boat?' she made herself ask, trying to sound as if that were her only concern.

'She's secure enough,' he responded easily. 'She's well roped, and there are two layers of truck tyre between her and the ramp. It's best to leave her there till daylight, when we can line her up properly for the winch.'

'Yes, I suppose so...'

'What made you stay?' he asked, his voice edged with sarcasm. 'Were you hoping for a touch of drama? A nice, juicy little news story to sell? I can't imagine it would hit the national headlines, a couple of lads adrift in a dinghy.'

She shook her head sadly. 'No. Getting a story isn't the only thing I ever think about—though I don't know what it will take to convince you.'

'So why did you stay?' he demanded in that hard, interrogatory tone which made her shiver.

'I... I was worried,' she admitted, finally bringing herself to turn her head, lifting her eyes to his. 'I went home, but I couldn't have slept so...I came back.'

'Why couldn't you have slept?'

Something beyond her will made her face him, made her put out one trembling hand to touch the hard wall of his chest, as if to make sure that he was real and solid, not some figment still lingering from her dreams. 'You know why,' she whispered.

He caught her wrist in a grip like steel, those stormy grey eyes as dark and dangerous as the sea. She drew in a sharp breath, recognising the glint of warning; some part of her urged escape, but as he moved closer, trapping her against the guard-rail, she knew that it was too late to run away—far too late...

She gasped as he dragged her fiercely into his arms, his mouth coming down to claim hers in a kiss that would brook no denial. But she wasn't thinking of denying him. His lips had crushed hers apart, his tongue ruthlessly plundering the sweet, secret depths of her mouth in a flagrantly sensual exploration that was setting her responses on fire. It was as if all the tension that had been sizzling between them since she had arrived at the cottage—since the first time they had met—had imploded into a force stronger than gravity itself, spinning her into a dizzying vortex, out of control.

The hunger inside her seemed to communicate itself to him, and as she wrapped her arms tightly around his neck he lifted her almost off her feet, curving her into the hard length of his body, making her devastatingly aware of the urgent demand that was as powerful and primeval as the thundering ocean beneath them.

For a moment he lifted his head, dragging in a harsh breath, a muttered curse in his throat. 'Damn you! I want you—I want you right now,' he grated, in a voice like the tearing of steel.

She stared up at him, shocked...knowing that her own need was as wild, as fevered as his. 'Yes,' she heard herself answer him. 'Yes—now!'

The flicker of flame in his eyes warned her that he had taken her at her word, but she had no chance to protest; his mouth had captured hers again. As she felt herself spun around she became aware of a slight lull in the wind, and realised that he had drawn her beneath the shelter of the boathouse, where the thick pylons that supported it were driven into concrete foundations abutting the raw granite cliffs.

He was crushing her against the jagged rock, but she didn't care—there was something in the savage intensity of his kiss that warned her that he would have no mercy. With swift impatience he had unfastened the buttons of her jacket, and then the ancient knitted cardigan she had thrown on for extra warmth. But as she realised that he was going to do the same with the woollen shirt beneath it, she remembered that in her hurry she hadn't bothered with a bra.

He was in no mood to be gentle as he stripped her clothing apart, his hands ruthless in their caresses as he savoured the soft silkiness of her skin. As he lifted his head she caught her breath on a sobbing moan, opening her eyes to see him gazing down at the ripe, creamy swell of her naked breasts, the dainty rosebud peaks puckering as they were exposed to the freezing sting of the night air. His laughter was lazily mocking; he knew that she was as helpless before the elemental force of his desire as a boat in a storm.

A larger wave crashed against the rocks below, and she felt the lash of ice-cold spray across her bare skin, but her gasp of shocked protest was stifled by his hot mouth on hers. His hands slid up to mould and caress the ripe firmness of her breasts, crushing them beneath his palms, rolling over the tender nipples with a heated friction, his clever fingers teasing and pinching at the hardened buds, starting a fire in her blood.

His oilskin jacket was unfastened, and beneath it she could see that his white silk shirt was open at the throat, showing a tempting glimpse of the rough curls that clustered across his wide chest. A vivid memory rose in her mind of that first night, when he had walked in and caught her in the shower; she had wanted then to run her palms over those hard ridges of muscle— and she wanted to now.

Her mind didn't even have to frame the conscious thought—her hands reached out of their own volition, fumbling with the awkward buttons, sliding inside to wrap around him and draw him against her, and with a sigh of pure pleasure she closed her eyes, resting her cheek against his warm skin, breathing in the subtle, musky scent of him, shivering at the delicious abrasion of that coarse male body-hair over her sensitised skin.

'Lynne...' She felt a shudder through his taut body, and then he grasped her shoulders, pinning her back against the cold rock wall behind her. 'This is crazy...'

'I know...'

His hands framed her face, his kisses dusting over her trembling eyelids, finding the pulse that beat wildly beneath her temple. 'If you don't stop me now...'

She gave herself a brief moment to see if there would be second thoughts, but there were none. In the cold light of morning she might regret this, but morning was still several hours away. 'I'm...not going to stop you,' she breathed.

She felt the soft hiss of his breath against her skin as he bent his head slowly into the hollow of her shoulder, his mouth hot as he traced a scalding path of kisses down the long, slender column of her throat. He lifted her to perch precariously against the rocks, and his hands moved to cup the aching swell of her breasts as if they were ripe peaches. He was lapping at the taut nipples with his rasping tongue, nipping lightly with his strong white teeth, sending sizzling sparks along her taut-strung nerve-fibres to scorch her brain.

She curled her fingers into his crisp dark blond hair, gazing out with dazed eyes at the wind-tossed waves, the moon-laced clouds racing across the dark sky. This had to be crazy, out here on a freezing night like this— they could at least have waited until they'd got back to the cottage and the comfort of a warm bed.

But she didn't care. And as he drew one succulent bud deep into his mouth and began to suckle at it with a strong, pulsing rhythm a sweet, piercing pleasure shafted right through her, curving her back into a quivering arch; the sobbing cry that broke from her lips echoed as if from a million miles away.

If she had had any doubt of his serious intent, it fled as she felt his hands on the snap of her jeans. She drew in a sharp breath, some last remnant of sanity reminding her that she shouldn't be letting him take her like this—so easy, so wild. But those stormy grey eyes were gazing down into hers, binding her with his spells, and they both knew she had no will to stop him as he dragged down the zip.

She surrendered on a whimpering sob of pleasure to the deep, hard thrust as he took her. She was clinging to him, insensible of the ice-cold wind or the sharp edges of rock digging into her shoulderblades. The storm was inside her now, raging in her blood, and she felt no shame at her own wantonness, making love like this, with this primitive urgency; she was too acutely aware that the cruel sea out there could have taken him, and she would never have got this chance.

It was too hot and fierce to last for more than a few minutes, but long before it was over Lynne knew that she had reached such soaring peaks of pleasure as she had never dreamed existed. As the last wild tremors shuddered through her she let go of her breath in a long, ragged sigh; whatever happened after this, it wouldn't matter—that one blissful moment of paradise had been worth any price she would have to pay.

With a low groan Rhys relaxed heavily against her, but then, with a consideration she hadn't really expected, he drew her jeans up again and wrapped her in his arms, his oilskin coat around them both as he protected her from the freezing night with the warmth of his body while their racing hearts gradually settled back to a normal, even beat.

Slowly reality began to seep back into her brain, and with it a somewhat belated sense of shame at what she had let him do to her. How *could* she...? Behaving with all the sophistication of a hormone-driven adolescent, out here on this open cliff-face beneath the shadow of the boathouse—except the local kids probably had the sense to come here only in decent weather!

But it was done now—she couldn't take it back. With her self-respect in tatters, there were really only two alternatives left to her: she could throw herself off the cliff right now, or she could try to act cool, as if it had been nothing of any significance—and she certainly wasn't going to choose the former.

She drew away from him, struggling for some semblance of dignity as she buttoned up her jacket. 'Well, I don't know about you, but I could do with a nice hot bath and a bowl of soup now. I'm afraid you'll have to make do with my car,' she added lightly, feeling in the pocket of her jacket for her car keys. 'I didn't fancy driving yours back down the hill.'

'That's OK,' he responded lazily. 'You can drive.'

'I wasn't thinking of offering to let you drive it anyway,' she rejoined, tossing the keys into the air and catching them again neatly.

'This isn't too bad.'

Lynne laughed a little unsteadily. 'Even I would find it difficult to make a mess of heating up a tin of soup,' she pointed out.

'I suppose so,' he conceded on a note of lazy humour.

They were sitting at the breakfast bar in the kitchen—and Lynne had managed to shift her stool discreetly as far away from him as possible. Rhys had taken his turn for a warm bath while she'd been heating the soup, and now he was wearing his dressing gown—a navy blue boxer's style hooded towelling robe. She had been reasonably all right till he had come downstairs in that, but now all she could think about was that rough scattering of dark curls across his wide chest, just visible in the shadow of the loose lapels.

He was watching her with that dark, perceptive gaze, and she shifted uncomfortably on her stool. 'So,' he remarked, 'you aren't writing about me.'

It was a statement, not a question, and she slanted him a swift glance. 'You finally believe me?'

He smiled slowly, his eyes teasing her. 'Even you wouldn't go as far as that to get a story,' he taunted. 'But, on the other hand, you're not writing a series of articles on career women for some new magazine either. So what *are* you writing?'

She felt a hot blush creep up over her cheeks. 'I... Actually I'm...trying to write a book,' she confessed a little sheepishly.

'A book?' He arched one level eyebrow in surprise. 'Why didn't you tell me that in the first place? Why all the secrecy?'

'It isn't going very well. I've only managed half a dozen pages since I got here.'

He laughed drily. 'I know the feeling.'

'You do? What do you do if it happens?'

'Write through it, or get up and do something else. But if you're having so much trouble with it right from the start, maybe you should just scrap it and start again.'

'I wondered about that,' she mused wryly. 'But I've been working on it for so long in my mind—a couple of years. I thought I had it all ready to set down on paper.'

He shook his head. 'It doesn't always work like that. Sometimes you can have a great idea, but it just doesn't play when you try to get it down on paper.' He picked up his bread roll and broke it in half, wiped it around his soup bowl to soak up the last dregs, and then with a sigh of satisfaction pushed the empty bowl away. 'Well, that's my stomach taken care of,' he teased, his eyes taking on a wicked glint as he stretched out his foot and ran it up the inside of her thigh. 'How about attending to my other appetites?'

Lynne felt a sudden wave of heat flood through her; unable to meet his eyes, she grabbed for the soup bowls and retreated quickly to the sink. Behind her she heard him laugh softly, mockingly.

'I thought you'd decided to stop playing games?' he taunted.

'I'm... I'm not playing games,' she returned, struggling to keep her voice steady. 'I just... Quite apart from anything else, you're still married.'

'Technically,' he conceded, an inflection of sardonic humour in his voice. 'Until next week. I've already instructed my solicitor to apply for the decree absolute as soon as it becomes available.'

'Well, but...even so...'

He had come up close behind her, trapping her against the sink. 'You know, for someone who professes to be against marriage, you seem to take it very seriously,' he remarked softly.

She moved cautiously away from him, shrugging her slender shoulders in a gesture of casual unconcern. 'I've never said I was against it as an institution,' she responded with studied indifference. 'It's just that...it isn't for me.'

He nodded agreement. 'That's good. I feel pretty much the same—having been through the mill once. It makes life a lot less complicated if neither of you has to pretend to some kind of everlasting commitment when all you're really looking for is a pleasant interlude.'

'Of course,' she conceded, struggling to keep her voice steady. 'Although... frankly, at the moment, I'm not particularly interested in a...casual sexual relationship either.'

'Oh?' Those dark eyes glinted with mocking amusement. 'And yet you seemed to be quite enjoying what we got up to underneath the boatshed—you didn't even seem to mind the cold. I haven't had a romp like that since I was in my teens, when there was nowhere else to go but round behind the gymnasium block at school. I have to admit, it was good fun.'

'So we both got a little...carried away,' she rejoined, trying to inject a note of worldly sophistication into her voice. 'It probably isn't surprising, after the past couple of weeks. It was no big deal.'

'No big deal?' He laughed softly, huskily, drawing her back against him, not bothering to ask permission to slide his hands up beneath her shirt to cup and mould the ripe swell of her breasts, still aching from his earlier caresses. He was teasing the exquisitely sensitised buds of her nipples, nipping and rolling them between his clever fingers, making her gasp in pleasure. 'Say that again now.'

Weakly she struggled against sweet temptation. 'I...'

He had bent his head and was nibbling lightly at the lobe of her ear, and she felt her bones turn to jelly. Unable to protest, she let him turn her in his arms, her lips parting as his mouth captured hers in a kiss of ruthless sensuality, his tongue plundering deep into the moist, sweet corners within. She could only curse her own weakness, which made it impossible for her to resist.

Her blood was racing in her veins, making her dizzy, so she had to lift her hands to grip the soft terry folds of his dressing gown, encountering the hard resilience of male muscle across his chest. The musky scent of his skin was drugging her mind, luring her towards a surrender she knew was reckless folly; this wasn't a dream from which she would wake in due course and then go about her day troubled by no more than a lingering, wistful memory—this was her life, and she was going to get her heart very seriously broken.

Gathering the last remnants of her strength, she drew back from him, though still held captive in his arms. 'I... I thought you were tired,' she protested a little shakily.

He smiled with lazy humour. 'I can sleep later. Right now I've got other things on my mind.'

And, before she had time to realise what he was going to do, he had hoisted her unceremoniously over his shoulder, ignoring her cry of furious protest as he carried her up the stairs, taking them two at a time. Reaching the landing, he nudged open the door of his bedroom and marched straight in, dumping her in a spitting, swearing heap in the middle of the big double bed.

'No big deal, huh? Don't you know how dangerous it is to challenge a man like that?'

He climbed onto the bed, kneeling across her thighs so that she couldn't escape, and, grasping both her wrists in one hand, reached across to the bedside table and picked up the silk bow-tie he had been wearing earlier. As her eyes widened in shock he wrapped it around her wrists, fastening them with ruthless efficiency to the brass frame of the bed behind her head.

'Hey!' she protested, trying to wriggle free. 'What do you think you're doing?'

'What does it look like I'm doing?' he responded on a husky, mocking laugh. 'Rules of war—make sure your prisoners can't escape before you start to...interrogate them.'

Slowly—achingly slowly—he began to unfasten the buttons down the front of her shirt. She drew in a deep, shaky breath, glaring up at him in angry defiance. But she was helpless, completely at his mercy—and the glint of wicked amusement in his eyes warned her unmistakably that he intended to take full advantage of her. And there was no way she could pretend, even to herself, that the fluttering sensation in the pit of her stomach was anything other than delicious anticipation.

'You might as well just relax and enjoy it,' he taunted, brushing the fabric aside to allow himself a free survey of her soft, naked curves. 'There's no escape—those knots are good and tight.'

'You louse,' she threw at him, refusing to let herself give in so easily.

He shook his head chidingly. 'Let's get one thing absolutely clear,' he murmured, a hint of genuine warning underlining the mocking amusement in his voice. 'The daylight hours you can devote to your career, and any...relationship we may have can take second place. But at night you're mine—every sweet, delicious inch of you.' He let his hands stroke lightly down over her body. 'You have such lovely skin—so smooth and silky. And such pretty little breasts—small, but as perfect as two ripe peaches.'

She had to bite her lip to stifle a moan of frustrated pleasure as with the very tip of one finger he traced a languid path round and round over the creamy contours, spiralling tantalisingly nearer and nearer to the taut rosebud peaks.

'And these,' he murmured, tipping each rose-pink nipple with his fingertips, 'are like sweet, juicy strawberries, just waiting to be plucked.' He caught the tender buds between his fingers and thumbs, pinching them lightly, tugging at them, rolling them around, and then he flattened his palms over them, crushing them deliciously.

She was losing the battle, betrayed by her own treacherous body, melting in helpless response, her breathing deep and ragged as she dragged for air, her spine curving as she writhed beneath him, tormented by the exquisite sensations rippling through her.

He laughed, that husky, sensuous laugh, low in his throat, and slowly bent his head first to one dainty nipple then the other, lapping at them with his hot tongue, swirling around them languorously, teasing them with his strong teeth, taking all the time in the world to savour his enjoyment of her body as she lay in a daze of mindless rapture, lost to everything but the incredible things he was doing to her.

He lifted his head, slanting her a mocking smile. 'Do you like that?' he taunted. 'Do you want me to go on?'

She caught her breath on a small sob of agony. He was going to insist on an answer, force her to admit to her own need. She gazed up into those hot grey eyes, losing herself in their hypnotic spell. Part of her still sought to defy him, but something much stronger was urging her towards the sweet surrender he was demanding. She closed her eyes, helpless to resist the temptation any longer. 'Yes,' she whispered raggedly. 'Yes, please...'

He growled in pleasurable satisfaction, bending his head once again to subject her to more of the sweet torment, this time taking one taut, ripe nipple deep into his mouth and suckling at it with a fierce, hungry rhythm that pulsed a primeval fever through her veins.

She longed to wrap her arms around him, to hold him to her, but the bonds around her wrists, though not tight, were very secure. Surely he knew by now that he had no need to keep her tied up in order to keep her in his bed? She suspected that he did, but this was something more—a symbolic demonstration of his power. He could do whatever he liked with her.

Kneeling up again, he smiled down at her in mocking satisfaction as one by one he unfastened the snaps of her jeans and then drew them slowly down over the slender length of her thighs. 'Do you know how long I've imagined myself doing this to you?' he queried, grinning wickedly. 'Right from that first time I saw you, that burning hot afternoon, spitting defiance at me outside the front gate of José's official residence. If I hadn't had José to get out of the country, I'd have dragged you off to my quarters right then and taught you not to be so damned insubordinate.'

She glanced up at him in surprise; so that frisson of

sexual tension hadn't been a figment of her imagination—he had felt it too.

He rose to his feet, laughing as he gazed down at her, naked now except for the tiny white lace triangle of her briefs. 'Mind you, even my most vivid fantasies could never conjure quite such an inviting prospect as this,' he taunted, his voice as smoky as the fire in his eyes. 'Such a delightful little plaything...warm and soft, and so delightfully willing. Though you really don't have much choice but to be willing at the moment, do you? Oh, don't waste your energy trying to get free,' he added as she sought once again to slip her wrists out of the bonds that were tying her to the bed. 'You won't manage it. You're my prisoner. It's a good job we had that little romp down by the boathouse to take the edge off my appetite—this is going to take a long, long time.'

Lynne lay watching him, her mouth dry. He had already shrugged his robe off his wide shoulders; he was wearing only a pair of silk-jersey boxers, dark green, and his lean, hard-muscled body was still touched bronze by the sun, the soft light of the bedside lamp sculpting its powerful male contours as if he were carved from golden marble.

'Wh-what are you going to do?' she pleaded, a little unsteadily.

'Oh, nothing you won't like,' he assured her on a husky laugh.

'How do I know that?'

The wicked glint in his eyes acknowledged the point as he moved back onto the bed. 'You'll just have to trust me, won't you?'

She drew in a sharp breath, her heartbeat fluttering as he caught one finger in the tight lacy fabric of her briefs to draw them down and cast them aside, leaving her completely naked. A small quiver of vulnerability ran through her, but she knew that she did trust him; more than that, she loved him. And she would do whatever he wanted her to do.

His eyes were watching her face as he trailed his hand lazily over her body, taking his time, caressing her with a slow, warm sensuality that was turning her bones to honey. And then he bent his head over her, dusting scalding kisses over her flushed skin, tasting every inch of her, from her temples to the tips of her toes. She closed her eyes, luxuriating in the strange, sweet rapture of it—he seemed to be discovering erogenous zones she had never known were there.

His touch was as smooth as silk as he stroked up over her thighs again, coaxing them apart to seek the most intimate caresses. 'Such velvet softness,' he murmured, exploring into the moist, delicate petals with gentle expertise. 'Like the heart of a full red rose.' He rewarded her compliance with a kiss, deep and intimately tender, swirling his tongue over all the sweet, sensitive membranes of her lips, stirring all the responses he was coming to know so well.

With unerring skill he found the tiny seed-pearl that was the focus of all her sensitised nerve-fibres, nestling in its secret fold, and as he stroked it a sizzling shock shafted through her, and she drew in her breath on a sobbing gasp, her spine a quivering arch. He was missing not one nuance of her response, tormenting her with the exquisite sensations until she was crying out, begging him incoherently for more of the same. If this was her punishment for insubordination she could only submit to it, straining helplessly against the bonds that held her prisoner as the pleasure racked her slender body.

She felt him move on the bed, and then to her shocked delight felt the heat of his mouth along the silken inner flanks of her thighs as he eased them wider apart, until his sensuous, rasping tongue took the place of his fingertip, languorously swirling over that acutely sensitive point, firing her blood with a fever that was scalding her brain.

By the time he finally returned to lie above her, she felt as if she could endure no more of this exquisite torture of pleasure. But as his mouth closed over hers again, his tongue plundering deep within, she knew that she could only surrender to his ultimate demand, and her thighs parted wider as she moved beneath him, offering her body in willing invitation to the first deep, powerful thrust as he took her.

'So,' he murmured, taunting her. 'No big deal?'

She peeped up at him from between her lashes, her blue eyes glowing. 'I'm sorry.'

'How sorry?'

Her smile was soft and sensual. 'Untie my hands and I'll show you.'

He laughed, finally accepting her plea, and she wrapped her arms around him, drawing him down to her, her heart and her soul yielding their last defences.

She could sense that he was restraining the driving forces inside him, taking care to hold his weight from her as he built the rhythm slowly, tantalising her, keeping his promise to make it last a long, long time. She had long passed the point of conscious awareness; wrapped in velvet darkness, she knew only the musky male scent of his body, the ragged sound of their breathing as the tension coiled inside her, hot and dangerous. She was moving with him, arching to meet the full measure of his demand, reckless of the warning tremors rippling through that powerful frame.

And then at last the control that had held him in check was overtaken by the sheer primitive force of his need, and he forgot to be gentle as he took his savage pleasure. She cried out in wild ecstasy, spinning in a dizzying vortex of fire as with a shuddering climax he thrust deep into her, a low growl of satisfaction escaping his throat as he collapsed beside her onto the pillow.

For a long time they lay, wrapped up in each other's arms. Lynne floated languidly in a golden sea, her body aching deliciously, her mind lost in a world of blissful half-sleep. She couldn't trust herself to speak in case the words that were seared into her heart came bubbling out. She loved him too much—far too much—to burden him with the guilt he would feel when the time came for him to move on. He wouldn't find it as easy to dump her as Paul had—he wasn't the kind. And that would only tarnish the memories of what they had had.

At last she realised that he had fallen asleep, still with his arms wrapped around her. With a small sigh she nestled against him, listening to the sound of his deep, steady breathing. She really ought to go back to her own room... But she suspected that if she tried to move he would wake, and stop her.

His prisoner... An odd little frisson of heat ran through her as she remembered the way he had made love to her, the lingering ache in her body recalling every touch, every deep thrust. His prisoner... Not that she would ever admit to him how close to the truth that was, of course. But as she drifted off into the realm of dreams a small smile was curving the corners of her soft lips.

CHAPTER TEN

'DON'T be stupid.' Lynne regarded her own tear-stained reflection in the bathroom mirror. 'You should be relieved, not bawling your eyes out. The last thing you need right now is to get pregnant.' That *would* have Rhys running for the hills—or, worse still, offering to marry her out of a misplaced sense of duty.

And, ironically, it wasn't really a baby she wanted—not right now, at least. Babies featured as some future part of the rose-tinted scenario her imagination created every time she let her guard slip for even an instant. It was becoming exhausting to have to keep a constant check on her emotions, never to let Rhys know that she had fallen deeply, helplessly, irrevocably in love with him.

She was going to have to leave. How many times had she told herself that in the past three months? February and March had slipped past almost without her noticing, and it was now the middle of April. And with every day she stayed it was getting more and more difficult to make the break. But if she didn't go soon she would find herself doing something stupid—like letting herself get pregnant, just so that she would always have some small part of him to keep when the dream was gone.

A splash of cool water soothed her tear-soaked eyes and took the betraying redness from her cheeks, but her bruised heart couldn't be so easily healed. She was going to have to leave—she repeated it to herself, almost like a mantra, as if that alone could give her the will-power she needed to make the break. She was going to have to leave.

By the time she went downstairs she was able to present her usual façade of breezy cheerfulness—although the sight of Rhys in the kitchen, cooking scrambled eggs, his long, lean legs moulded by the faded denim of his ancient jeans, his feet bare, made her heart flutter as fast as it had the very first time she had met him.

'Coffee?' He greeted her with his sensuous morning smile, satisfied after another long night of making love.

'Uh-huh.' She strolled over to the kitchen table and picked up the post, shuffling through it quickly to separate out any that were addressed to her. There were three: her bank statement, an offer to scratch a card and win a car from some mail-order company, and a letter from her old paper. She slit the envelope open and scanned the contents, laying it aside as Rhys brought her coffee to the table.

'Good morning,' he murmured, bending over her to claim her mouth in a long, deep, intimate kiss. 'Do you want toast with your breakfast?'

'Please.' She smiled up at him; somehow he managed to look incredibly sexy, padding around the kitchen in his bare feet, his hair still damp from his shower, expertly whipping together the kind of breakfast a five-star hotel would have been proud of.

They had agreed originally that they would share the cooking, but within a couple of days he had declared that if he was going to survive he would have to take it over—a suggestion she had been delighted to accede to. The down-side was that she was supposed to do all the washing up—she had lately begun to consider the advantages of buying a dishwasher.

'Are you...planning to work today?' she asked him. She had been trying not to notice how, over the past few weeks, the stack of paper on his desk that represented the main draft of his novel—annotated and scribbled all over with red pen—was now less than a quarter of an inch thick. He must be down to the last couple of chapters—if that.

'I'll do a couple of hours before lunch,' he responded, getting the butter out of the fridge. 'I promised to go out with Curran this afternoon and give him a hand checking the buoys over that old wreck down by Castle Head.'

She nodded. She was getting a little too used to this—sitting opposite him at the breakfast table, reading the post or the morning paper, the radio playing, discussing their plans for the day. It was beginning to feel like the normal pattern of her life—and that was dangerous.

Already there were signs down in the village that the season was beginning to get underway. Shops were getting ready to open, boats were being painted, and there were strange cars inching their way along the harbour-front and strange faces in the Smuggler's Rest. With the return of the men who had been working away for the winter the lifeboat crew was up to its full strength of fourteen again. Soon the place would be full of tourists—and she couldn't imagine that Rhys would want to stay. Summer was coming. It was just a question of which of them would fly away first.

Rhys had opened one of his letters—Lynne's curiosity had been pricked by the envelope, of thick cream vellum addressed in an elegant, almost certainly feminine hand—and now he laughed aloud as he skimmed through its contents. 'Well, well—old Nine-Bob Nigel! I never thought he had it in him!' he chuckled.

'Who?'

'It's from Helena,' he responded, holding up the letter. 'She's getting married again.'

'Oh. . .?' Her heart gave a sharp thud. 'That was quick.'

'Wasn't it just? Trust Helena not to let the grass grow under her feet. Poor old Nige—he wouldn't have stood a chance.'

'Why did you call him "Nine-Bob Nigel"?' she asked.

'That was what we used to call him at school. He wasn't too bright academically—a little short of the full ten-shilling note, as it were. But he's a nice enough chap. Filthy rich, of course, and heir to an earldom, complete with stately home. Helena will love that—

playing lady of the manor and swanning around with everyone calling her Countess.'

He didn't sound too concerned—it was almost as if he were speaking of a sister or a cousin rather than his ex-wife. 'You...don't mind?' she queried carefully.

He shrugged those wide shoulders in a gesture of casual unconcern. 'He'll probably make her a far better husband than I ever did. Poor old Helena—I'm afraid our marriage was a severe disappointment to her.'

She slanted him a searching look from beneath her lashes. The question of his marriage had been in her mind for a long time—could she risk asking it now. 'Why...did you marry her?' she ventured warily.

He smiled a little crookedly. 'Oh, I suppose I must have thought I was in love with her at the time. After all, she's beautiful, charming, intelligent—what more could I have asked for?' His voice was laced with bitter self-mockery. 'Unfortunately life—marriage—didn't turn out to be quite as simple as I'd anticipated.'

No, Lynne acknowledged wryly—life so rarely did. And it really wasn't surprising that after such a disastrous experience of marriage he would be in no hurry to try it again. She had known that from the beginning, of course—he had been quite honest about it. And to be fair, she had made every effort to convince him that she felt exactly the same. It was a little too late now to tell him that what she really wanted was the 'happy ever after' bit, the ride off into the sunset hand in hand as the violins played.

'What was your letter?' he enquired.

'Oh...it's from my old paper.'

'About your unfair dismissal case?'

'Sort of. Actually, they're offering to settle.' She had to remind herself to inject a suitable degree of enthusiasm into her voice. 'Apparently Paul's gone. They say he left "by mutual agreement"—which probably means he got fired—though it doesn't say why. Anyway, they "regret the circumstances" of my dismissal, and they're offering me my old job back—at a higher salary and with my own by-line. Plus compensation for loss of earnings.'

'That sounds like a pretty good offer,' he accorded. 'Congratulations—you won.'

'Thank you.' Her smile was bright, though her heart was breaking. She had to go—she couldn't stay. 'They. . .they want me back next week.'

'So soon? What about finishing your book?'

'Oh. . .I. . .might as well put that on hold for a while. I can always finish it off later.' Though she knew she never would; it was too much a part of her life down here—she would never be able to recapture the inspiration anywhere else. 'I could leave the day after tomorrow, and stay with Carole until I find a place of my own. The compensation might even be enough to put the deposit on a flat.'

Those grey eyes gave nothing away but a glint of mocking amusement. 'Can't wait to get back to the rat race, eh? Life too peaceful for you down here?'

'Ah, well—you know how it is. I suppose I'm too much of a city girl at heart—I miss the buzz.'

'And the crowds, and the traffic, and the pollution. . .' he added drily.

She shrugged such drawbacks aside with a lift of her slender shoulders, although she was beginning to realise—perhaps for the first time—how little she had really missed her old way of life, with its constant pressure to beat the clock, or the opposition, or some unrealistic target set by a little man in a grey suit who only understood profit margins.

Funny—she had thought Rhys was the only reason she wanted to stay down here, but he wasn't; there were so many more reasons. She liked being able to smell the sea instead of diesel fumes; she liked pavements strewn with buttercups instead of discarded polystyrene cartons from the fast-food emporium on the corner; she liked shopping at a market where the stallkeepers knew her name and which kind of breakfast cereal she liked, instead of queuing at a supermarket checkout where some gum-chewing teenager was more interested in discussing last night's telly with her friend on the next till than in dealing with the customers.

And she liked weaving fantasy tales of piskies and giants, of brave maidens and warrior knights, which seemed to spin out of her head like silver threads and bore no relation whatsoever to the grubby menu of sleaze and scandal that made up too large a part of the daily diet of a newspaper journalist.

When had it happened, this sea change? She hadn't noticed... Perhaps it had been there beneath the surface for a long time—far longer than she had suspected. But it was her misfortune that she hadn't realised it until now, when it was too late. She couldn't stay, just waiting for the time to come when Rhys would say he was going—at least this way she could walk away with her head held high and a crumb of self-respect.

'There—I think that's the lot.' Lynne held down the contents of her big nylon sports-bag with one hand while drawing round the zip with the other. 'If you find anything I've forgotten, could you send it on to me?'

'Of course.'

She was getting quite good at keeping up a cool façade, she reflected wryly. And if some foolish part of her had been hoping Rhys would ask her to stay, she would have been seriously disappointed. His only response to the announcement of her departure had been to ask her if she and Carole would be willing to sell him the cottage.

She had been only too happy to agree on her own behalf—she would never come back here anyway—and Carole too, shrewd and sympathetic, hadn't asked any awkward questions, but had consented to the sale. The money would come in handy, of course—with the compensation she was due from the paper, she would be able to find somewhere quite decent to live in London.

'Well...that's it, then.' Somehow she managed a smile. 'I'd better be off—I want to get a good start, in case the car decides to play me up.' She swung the bag over her shoulder and then hesitated, uncertain. He was standing in the bedroom doorway, leaning one wide shoulder negligently against the jamb, watching her, those cool grey eyes giving absolutely nothing away. Would he kiss her goodbye? And if he did, would she still be able to leave?

'Mind how you go.' He glanced up at the window as the wind rattled rain against the glass. 'You haven't exactly picked the best day for driving.'

'No—it's more like November than April, isn't it? But I have to get back today—I'll need a day or two to sort things out before I go back to work on Monday. Are you...going to wish me luck?'

'Of course,' he responded with a laconic smile. 'Not that you need it—you'll knock 'em dead.'

'Thank you.' She smiled back; it had been meant as a genuine compliment, one she would have valued highly just a few short months ago, but it wasn't what she wanted to hear him say; she wanted to hear him say, Don't go.

'So...' He reached out with a confident hand and drew her against him. 'It's been good.' His breath was warm on her upturned face as he gazed down at her, as if considering exactly where he was going to kiss her.

'Yes...' Her heart wasn't so much breaking as being painfully cut into small pieces with a dull knife.

His mouth brushed lightly over hers, warm and intimate, reminding her achingly of all the kisses they had shared—was this really the very last one? With a low groan she dropped her bag and wrapped her arms around his neck, curving herself close against him, her lips parting in pleading invitation. And he responded, his tongue deeply plundering all the sweet, secret corners within, stirring responses that no one else ever had—ever could—arouse.

If she could only make time stand still, right now, stay for ever in his arms... Hot tears had welled into her eyes and were spilling over her cheeks as he kissed her, their salt taste trickling into her mouth. But she couldn't hold them back. By tomorrow, would she even be able to remember exactly what it felt like to be held like this, to recapture in her mind that faint, musky, male scent of his skin, the feel of his curling hair between her fingers?

He lifted his head, one dark eyebrow raised in quizzical enquiry as he looked down at her. She drew back, scrubbing the back of her hand across her eyes as she struggled to present a smile. 'I'm sorry—I hate goodbyes,' she managed limply. 'Perhaps I'd better just get going.'

'Perhaps you had,' he conceded, a sardonic edge in his voice, and, picking up her bag, he waited for her to precede him down the stairs.

She had always felt a certain sadness when leaving the cottage, but it had always been tempered by the knowledge that she would be coming back. But this was the last time—for ever. She glanced around wistfully at the cosy rooms with their old-fashioned furniture; there would be so many memories to haunt her...

The wind swirled rain into their faces as they opened the front door. 'I hope your windscreen wipers are working properly,' Rhys said, ducking his head into his shoulders as he ran down the steps to throw her bag onto the back seat of her car with the rest of her stuff.

'Yes, they are—don't worry,' she assured him, scrambling in behind the wheel to get out of the rain. But then she was sorry she had been so quick—rain or no rain, she might have had one last hug, one last kiss before she drove away. She squinted up at him as he leaned over the open door, her smile a little crooked. 'Well...goodbye, then.'

'Goodbye.' His hair was wet, one sparkling diamond

of rain about to drip from the darkened blond curl across his forehead, but he leaned into the car, his hand touching hers where it rested on the wheel, his mouth brushing hers, too briefly—much too briefly. 'Take care of yourself. Maybe I'll see you some time when I'm up in London.'

'Yes—that would be nice.' So casual, so cool, when what she really wanted to do was throw herself into his arms and beg him never to let her go. 'I'll probably be at Carole's for a couple of weeks, until I find myself somewhere, so if you do find anything I've left behind...'

'I'll send it on,' he promised again, and let the car door swing shut, standing back to watch as she reversed carefully out of the space next to his Jaguar and manoeuvred round in a three-point turn to drive away up the narrow lane. The last she saw of him was as he paused on the doorstep, his hand raised in a final wave of farewell, before disappearing into the cottage and closing the door.

The windscreen wipers were clacking briskly across the glass, sweeping away the pouring rain, but it was still difficult to see—her eyes were too full of tears. Reaching into her handbag, she pulled out a tissue and tried to dab them away, but King Canute would have had about as much success in trying to turn back the tide.

The harbour, which had begun to look so bright and summery, seemed to have sunk back into its winter sleep—only the little shop next to the Smuggler's Rest was still making an effort to look lively: the carousels of postcards on the pavement outside swathed in polythene bags to keep them dry, the red and yellow beach balls slung in string bags in the doorway bouncing in the wind. No one would be playing with beach balls on a day like this.

She had to drive carefully over the wet cobbles and then coax the little car up the steep hill on the far side, out of the village. The houses gave way to trees, and then she was up on the cliff road, able to see out over the open sea beyond the headland.

She caught her breath at the sight of it; she hadn't realised it would be so rough—after all it was the middle of April. But that meant nothing—the sea was the sea: wild and dangerous, subject to no laws but its own. Through the slanting sheets of rain she could see the white tops of the waves breaking all the way out to the horizon—it was almost as bad as the night she had arrived.

In spite of the rain, she couldn't resist the temptation to stop the car at the same place, that little lay-by at the bend in the road, where the first glimpse—or the last—could be caught of the village below. Anyway, she needed to wait for a little while until she could manage to stop crying, otherwise she wouldn't be safe to drive.

At least it was the right kind of weather to suit her mood—it would have been so much harder to leave on a sunny day, when the sea was sparkling blue and the piquant scent of wild gorse was in the air. The turbulent grey ocean matched the bitter emotions in her heart perfectly. Was it really just a little over three months since that stormy night when she had driven down here from London? It felt like years...or just moments. But at least for that short period of time she had lived her dream—not many people could say that.

She finally gave up the struggle, leaning back in her seat and letting the tears stream down her face as the rain streamed down the windscreen of the car. It was better this way—she had to keep reminding herself of that. If he had cared, even just a little bit, he wouldn't have let her go.

It was a long time before she felt ready to set off again, but she really couldn't sit here all day. With a last snuffle she blew her nose, and, sighing in sad resignation, leaned forward to start the ignition. The stupid thing fired first time, as if eager to be gone, and, checking briefly over her shoulder that there was nothing behind her on the road, she pulled out of the lay by...

The characteristic 'zip' of maroons streaking up into the sky from the harbour below startled her. As the twin bangs echoed along the cliffs her breath seemed to stop in her throat. The lifeboat had been called out—and Rhys would be going with it.

Without even thinking about it, she swung the wheel, turning the car back the way she had come. There was no way she could drive away knowing that he was out there on that unforgiving ocean. Of course, she had known that there would be times when he would be going out again, when she wouldn't be there, but that was different—she wouldn't have actually *known* when he was out. She couldn't leave until she knew that he was safe.

It was difficult to make herself drive slowly enough to be sure of keeping control of the steering on the steep, wet road when her heart was racing so swiftly ahead. When she came back up the hill from the harbour to the triangular-shaped space in front of the boathouse there was the usual jumble of cars and bicycles, but she saw the dark green Jaguar without even looking for it.

She slewed the little Citroën into a gap and jumped out, not even bothering to lock the door. But as she dashed into the boathouse she knew that she was just seconds too late—the boat was already at the bottom of the slipway, and she was in time only to see the surging wave as she plunged into the water before rising under her own super-buoyancy and setting course for the open sea.

'Oh...' She hadn't even caught a glimpse of him. Already the shore-crew were tidying up, and Barney grinned as he caught sight of her.

'Hello, there, lovey. Thought you was off up to London today?'

She shook her head, smiling wryly. 'I was on my way

when I heard the maroons. What's the call about, do you know?'

Barney's expression darkened. 'It's one o' them Liberian-registered crates—bulk carrier,' he told her grimly. 'Got a fire in the engine room. Sailor's nightmare, that—a fire at sea. They might have to go in and try and take the crew off her.'

Lynne felt cold fingers of fear wrap themselves around her heart. 'Couldn't...couldn't that be dangerous?' she enquired, trying hard to keep her voice steady.

'Aye—more than a bit,' Barney conceded. He glanced at his watch, checking it against the clock on the wall. 'Ten twenty-five. I'd better get the log opened. Want to put the kettle on, lovey?'

'Yes, I will.' She was glad of the comfort of the routine; there had been two or three genuine shouts for the boat over the past couple of months, as well as the regular training exercises, and each time she had stayed here at the boathouse with Barney, making tea and listening to his salty tales, and generally keeping him company through the long watch until the boat came home. She was glad not to have to explain to him why she was staying this time too.

Lynne sat and watched wearily as the hands of the clock ticked slowly round to nine o'clock. The boat had been out all day, joined now by the boat from Padstow, as well as the Sea Kings from Culdrose, and they were all still trying to get the men off the stricken freighter as the tugs fought a steadily losing battle to keep it from being driven onto the rocks.

She felt so helpless, able only to sit here safe on the shore and listen to what was going on out there. There had been a heart-stopping moment of terror a few hours earlier when, trying to manoeuvre around the giant stern of the ship more than a hundred times their size, the lifeboat had been caught broadside-on by a huge wave and had almost capsized. She had heard only the yelling and clattering over the short-wave radio, and her stomach had clenched in fear—until to her relief she had heard Rhys's voice, grumbling that he'd spilled his soup. Fortunately no one had been on deck at that moment—safe inside the cabin, with the seal-door shut, the crew had suffered no more than a few bruises.

From time to time the wives and girlfriends of the other crew members had come down to find out what was happening, and had stayed for a while, but she and Barney had the boathouse to themselves again now. It had stopped raining for a while during the afternoon, but it had started once more, and the wind was gusting up to a fierce nine or ten, which had forced the helicopters to break off and return to base.

'More tea?' she suggested to Barney, watching with sympathy as he ran his hand across his tired old eyes.

'Thanks, lovey. I don't know what I'd do without you here.'

She smiled at him a little awkwardly. 'You managed before I came.'

'Aye. But I've kind of got used to having you around now. It's good to have the company.'

She said no more, but made the tea and then settled down again in the chair beside Barney's desk to listen to that distant, metallic voice which was her only link to the man she loved with every beat of her heart.

It was almost an hour later when there was another flurry of activity. Lynne had been dozing, but was woken by Rhys's voice, yelling to his opposite number on the other lifeboat. 'Damn—the tide's turning. The tugs'll never hold her now... Look out—she's swinging round!'

There was a buzz of white noise while she and Barney leaned close to the short-wave, trying to hear what was being said. 'What's going on?' she queried, frowning.

'Seems like the Padstow boat's taken a clip from the anchor chain as the tide turned the freighter—damaged their wheelhouse, though no one's hurt, the Lord be praised. They're going to take on the lads our boys have already got and head for home.'

'But what about our boat?' Lynne protested a little desperately. 'They've been out there for almost twelve hours. They must be exhausted.'

'The captain and the bosun are still on board the carrier—they have to get them off. They're going through the slot—under the lee of the boat, between her and the rocks. It's the only chance they've got.' Barney drew in a long, deep breath and sat down. 'Heaven help them.'

Lynne had thought she knew all about worrying, but the next few minutes, as she sat chewing the knuckle of her thumb, listening helplessly to the sounds of what was taking place out there on the dark, treacherous ocean, were the worst nightmare she had ever had to live through.

It was impossible to tell exactly what was happening—all she could hear was a confusing mêlée of shouts, occasionally recognisable as Rhys's voice or sometimes Curran's. If only her imagination weren't quite so vivid, painting all too realistically the scene, with the huge dark hull of the freighter looming over the tiny lifeboat and the steep waves breaking against the razor-backed rocks in a cauldron of white foam not fifty yards away.

Suddenly a cheer went up, and as Lynne felt her head spin with relief she heard Rhys's voice again through the crackle of static. 'Porthwyk lifeboat to MR Sub. We've got them—repeat, crew all evacuated. The salvage boys can have what's left of this in the morning—we're clearing off. Over and out.' A few seconds later she heard him again, much more distinctly. 'Porthwyk lifeboat to shore-base. You awake, Barney? Get the kettle on—we're coming home.'

Barney chuckled, flicking the radio to 'transmit'. 'Shore-base to Porthwyk lifeboat. The kettle's already on. She makes a good cup of tea, your lass. Over.'

There was a brief pause before Rhys spoke again,

slowly, almost warily. 'You mean she's there with you now? Over.'

'Of course she is.' Barney winked at her, his eyes dancing. 'She's been here all day. Over.'

Again there was a pause, even longer, and Lynne stared at the radio, wishing she could see his face. But all he said was, 'Tell her to stay there till I get back. Over and out.'

The flashing blue light on the roof of the lifeboat appeared around the headland and a ragged cheer went up from the small crowd that had gathered in the past half-hour; half the village seemed to have turned out to welcome the brave crew home. There was an ambulance waiting too, as well as the hack from the local paper—and even some of the early tourists, their video cameras taking in every detail as the sleek blue and orange boat steered its careful course into the harbour.

It had stopped raining and the wind had dropped; it had been a long wait, but at last it was over. Leaning on the window-sill of the boathouse, Lynne watched as a couple of the shore-crew ran down the ramp to catch the ropes as they were thrown from the deck, and the weary crew trudged up the long steps to the boathouse.

Not entirely sure of what to expect from Rhys, she hung back a little as the others surged forward, wives greeting husbands with hugs and tears of relief. The two men who had been the last to be taken off the freighter were led away to the ambulance, drawing off the reporter and most of the tourists, thinning out the crowd that had been hiding her just as Rhys stepped through the boathouse door.

He paused, leaning one wide shoulder against the frame, those dark eyes regarding her with a glint of lazy mockery—and something else that made her heart turn over. 'So, you're back. Even sooner than I expected.'

She stared up at him, faintly bewildered. 'You *knew* I'd come back?'

'Of course.' He smiled that wide, wonderful smile. 'You don't think I'd have let you walk away from me if I hadn't been sure of that, do you?'

'I... But... You never said anything,' she protested weakly.

'What did you expect me to say?' He reached out and caught her hand, drawing her towards him. 'You were telling the whole world your career came first—I thought I'd just better wait until you'd worked out for yourself that what you really want is to be my wife.'

She felt a hot blush of pink rise to her cheeks and shook her head quickly, trying to draw back from him. 'Oh... No... You...don't have to marry me,' she insisted, a little breathless. 'I just... We can just be together...for as long as you want.'

He laughed, drawing her inexorably into the circle of his strong arms. 'I'm too tired to argue with you right now,' he growled on a flicker of impatience. 'Maybe this'll convince you.'

His mouth came down on hers in a kiss so fierce and hungry that there could be no resistance. Her lips parted in sweet surrender and his hand slid down the length of her spine to curve her slender body indecently close against his, warning her quite unmistakably that, tired as he might be, he still had the strength to assert his desires.

By the time he finally let her go, there was no way she could deny him anything. Shyly she peeped up at him from beneath her lashes. 'I... I didn't think you'd want to get married again,' she murmured shyly. 'I mean...after...Helena.'

He smiled down at her, his arms still holding her loosely around the waist. 'I should never have married Helena,' he acknowledged wryly. 'I didn't really love her—any more than she loved me. The odd thing is, I'd finally made up my mind to ask her for a divorce—but she beat me to it and asked me for a divorce instead.'

Her eyes widened in surprise. 'You were going to ask *her* for a divorce?'

He nodded. 'I suppose I should have done it a long time ago, but...it had never seemed very important. We were living virtually separate lives anyway, and I'd grown too cynical to believe in miracles. Until one day something totally unexpected happened—something that made me realise that life could still have the odd miracle in store, even for me.'

'Oh?'

His eyes took on a gleam of pleasant reminiscence. 'I'd fallen head over heels in love with a feisty little half-pint blonde that I'd only known for a couple of hours—and not in the most romantic of circumstances. Of course, it was pretty lousy timing—even if you hadn't been already spoken for, there wasn't a great deal I could do under those circumstances. But I figured that if a thunderbolt could hit me once, it could hit me again.'

She lifted her eyes to gaze up at him. 'You fell in love with me then?' she queried, bemused. 'I had no idea. I didn't even think you *liked* me.'

'I didn't say I liked you.' His mouth curved into a grim smile. 'You were a damned nuisance—distracting me from what I was supposed to be concentrating on. And as a result I damned nearly got you killed.' His hold on her tightened convulsively. 'I told myself I wasn't letting you leave with José because you'd stop at the first telex office you found and fax the news through to London—but the truth was that I wanted to keep you with me just for that little extra time that I had.'

Lynne laughed softly, leaning her cheek against the hard wall of his chest, a small glow of happiness warming through her. 'But if I hadn't been there when you got shot you might have died,' she reminded him. 'Anyway, you were even more horrible to me at Carole's dinner party.'

'True.' He smiled down at her crookedly. 'I wasn't in the best frame of mind at the time. My leg was giving me hell, and I was wondering if I was going to be able to live up to all the hype my first book had stirred up. Then, when I found out that the sister Carole had been so keen for me to meet was a journalist, I thought I was being set up to agree to giving an exclusive interview. When it turned out to be you I wasn't quite sure how I wanted to react.'

'Nor was I,' Lynne admitted wryly. 'I thought I'd really blown it that night—I didn't think I'd ever see you again.'

'Oh, I don't think your matchmaking sister would have given up that easily,' he assured her with a grin. 'But it was pretty obvious you were still screwed up over breaking up with your fiancé—I didn't think you'd be too keen to get involved with anyone else for a while, so I decided not to push it until you were a little more...receptive.'

'Instead of which, when you found me in your bed you promptly ordered me out!' she reminded him, laughing.

'It came as something of a shock to find you there,' he countered. 'And I wasn't about to let the way I felt about you interfere with my natural caution. Unfortunately, the way I felt about you proved rather too strong to control...' he added, bending his head to claim her mouth again in a warm, wonderful kiss...

'Are you two going to stand there canoodling all day?' came Curran's dry voice from behind them. 'Only we're about ready to lock up the boathouse—if it isn't too inconvenient?'

'We are not canoodling!' Rhys protested in a show of mild indignation.

'Looks like it to me,' Curran insisted. 'If you two are finally fixing to set the wedding bells ringing, I hope you won't forget to invite me.'

'You'd better be there,' Rhys retorted. 'You're going to be the best man.'

The coxswain grinned broadly. 'You're on! Now get a shift on out of here—I want to get home to my bed.'

'So do I,' Rhys agreed, slanting Lynne a look of wicked amusement.

'I thought you were tired?' she protested, her cheeks blushing a delightful shade of pink.

He drew her close into the possessive circle of his arms. 'Not too tired to make love to you,' he assured her huskily. 'I'll never be too tired for that.'

MILLS & BOON

Next Month's Romances

Each month you can choose from a wide variety of romance novels from Mills & Boon. Below are the new titles to look out for next month from the Presents and Enchanted series.

Presents™

CRAVING JAMIE	Emma Darcy
THE SECRET WIFE	Lynne Graham
WEDDING DAZE	Diana Hamilton
KISS AND TELL	Sharon Kendrick
MARRYING THE ENEMY!	Elizabeth Power
THE UNEXPECTED CHILD	Kate Walker
WEDDING-NIGHT BABY	Kim Lawrence
UNGENTLEMANLY BEHAVIOUR	Margaret Mayo

Enchanted™

THE SECOND BRIDE	Catherine George
HIS BROTHER'S CHILD	Lucy Gordon
THE BADLANDS BRIDE	Rebecca Winters
NEEDED: ONE DAD	Jeanne Allan
THE THREE-YEAR ITCH	Liz Fielding
FALLING FOR THE BOSS	Laura Martin
THE BACHELOR PRINCE	Debbie Macomber
A RANCH, A RING AND EVERYTHING	Val Daniels

Available from WH Smith, John Menzies, Volume One, Forbuoys, Martins, Woolworths, Tesco, Asda, Safeway and other paperback stockists.

KEEPING COUNT

How would you like to win a year's supply of Mills & Boon® books? Well you can and they're FREE! Simply complete the competition below and send it to us by 31st October 1997. The first five correct entries picked after the closing date will each win a year's subscription to the Mills & Boon series of their choice. What could be easier?

$$6 + 3 + \square = 14$$

$$\square + 2 + \square = 15$$

$$\square + 1 + \square = 16$$

$$\square + 6 + \square = 17$$

$$\square + 3 + \square = 18$$

$$\square + 1 + \square = 19$$

$$\square + 5 + \square = 20$$

C7D

PLEASE TURN OVER FOR DETAILS OF HOW TO ENTER ☞

How to enter...

There are six sets of numbers overleaf. When the first empty box has the correct number filled into it, then that set of three numbers will add up to 14. All you have to do, is figure out what the missing number of each of the other five sets are so that the answer to each will be as shown. The first number of each set of three will be the last number of the set before. Good Luck!

When you have filled in all the missing numbers don't forget to fill in your name and address in the space provided and tick the Mills & Boon® series you would like to receive if you are a winner. Then simply pop this page into an envelope (you don't even need a stamp) and post it today. Hurry, competition ends 31st October 1997.

Mills & Boon 'Keeping Count' Competition
FREEPOST, Croydon, Surrey, CR9 3WZ

Eire readers send competition to PO Box 4546, Dublin 24

Please tick the series you would like to receive if you are a winner
Presents™ ❑ Enchanted™ ❑ Temptation® ❑
Medical Romance™ ❑ Historical Romance™ ❑

Are you a Reader Service Subscriber?   Yes ❑   No ❑

Ms/Mrs/Miss/Mr_____
(BLOCK CAPS PLEASE)

Address _____

_____

_____ Postcode _____

(I am over 18 years of age)

One application per household. Competition open to residents of the UK and Ireland only.
You may be mailed with other offers from other reputable companies as a result of this application. If you would prefer not to receive such offers, please tick box. ❑

C7D